ETERNITY

Eternity

GREEN CITY BOOKS
Bend, OR

ISBN: 9781963101027
FIRST EDITION
designed by Isaac Peterson
cover photography by Isaac Peterson
Library of Congress Cataloging-in-Publication Data has been applied for.

23 24 LSC 10 9 8 7 6 5 4 3 2 1

Also by David Plante

ETERNITY

A NOVEL

DAVID PLANTE

FOR JOSEPH OLSHAN

One

He knew it from the past, from when he had once walked along the same street in the town of clapboard houses with lawns and decorative shrubs, there where he grew up with his American longing to go away, an especially American longing when you were alone at dusk walking along an American street, and no lights lit in the dusk.

Someone was playing a piano, and this surprised him, that anyone at all in Revere, Massachusetts, was playing the piano. He stopped to listen, and he thought that here he was, and it was as though he had never left, that as a teenager he had stood here and had heard someone play the piano, and he recalled there had come to him then the longing for all that he could not have. And back then as now the sound of a piano playing in a dark house was unbearable to him. The piano playing ceased, and a light came on through a window in the bungalow.

He longed for London, he longed for Hilary, in London.

Two

Theodore Beauchemin lay on his parents' bed, where they had died.

He lay for a long while, but he was there to look through the drawers that he had not been allowed to look into when he was a boy, so he made himself get up, and from a drawer in a wardrobe he took out a metal box, and sitting now on the edge of the bed, he put it on his lap. It was rectangular, green, somewhat dented, and had a hasp and a staple but no padlock.

Ted lifted the lid of the metal box and he saw a large birthday card, laminated, with a picture of a lilac bush in full bloom. He opened the card and under a printed poem wishing her a happy birthday, he read a message in his father's handwriting, a message to his mother, addressing her with a name he had never heard his father use for her.

You're my funny face.

He hadn't known his parents had had a relationship that was so light-spirited.

Beneath the card were more cards, birthday cards and anniversary cards and thank-you cards, all saved, Ted thought, by his mother, who

would have saved them as small expressions of
her friends' attention to her.

Ted threw the unread cards into a wastepaper basket. He was looking quickly through the
strong box for legal documents, one of which
was as an insurance policy against his own young
death, and too outdated to be of any worth.
Whenever he did come across documents which
might have been of interest, he collected them together to give to the lawyer.

Toward the bottom of the strong box were
letters. From the handwriting of the names and
addresses on the envelopes, he knew they were
letters written by his parents to each other. The
dates showed that they had been married when
they wrote the letters, and the dates showed that
they had been separated before Ted was born and
came together when he was born. He spread these
letters out on his parents' bed to study them,
picking up one envelope after another to look
closely at the dates, franked in little blue-black
circles on the old stamps. The return addresses
on the back flaps were different, so his parents
had lived apart for a time, and the letters were
written, yes, before his birth.

He gathered the letters together to decide
what to do with them. How could he bring himself to read them? How could he read into his

parents a past about something that they had never mentioned to him, a separation he knew nothing about? They had kept the letters, thinking, he supposed, that the letters were in a place he was not allowed to look into. And over the years of being together, years of Ted's growing, they had forgotten about them.

He took up the first envelope from the small stack, one on which he saw his father's handwriting addressing his mother, and he slid the letter out and unfolded it.

Oh, my darling, I miss you so much, so much, so much.

Ted could not bear this. No, he could not bear to continue to read. He could not bear to read any other letters. He folded the letter and placed it back into the envelope, and he gathered all the envelopes and lifted them and lowered them, again and again, as if to weigh their contents against what he didn't know about his parents and, perhaps, what he shouldn't know.

But he read a letter from his mother to his father.

Oh, my love—

No, he couldn't bear this. He folded this letter.

Ted threw them all into the wastepaper basket. He wouldn't read them. No, he couldn't read them, he couldn't bear reading letters his parents sent to each other from either side of a separa-tion. They longed for each other, a longing which finally brought them together in the birth of their son, Ted, their only child.

He closed the metal box, held it on his lap, and thought he wouldn't continue looking through the contents, for what else could he find that so struck him, that so upset him?

Under a long, brown envelope with the name of the insurance company printed on its upper left- hand corner, Ted found this photograph:

It was of him, of him aged seven, thirty years before, when he had received his Holy Communion.

But this boy, dressed in white and holding his Holy Communion prayer book, couldn't have been him, couldn't be him, Ted, now, but some other Ted, for whom the meaning of receiving the host was the boy's and had no meaning for the present Ted.

Ted no longer knew that past Ted, but he could look at the boy with the wonder of not knowing him. The Ted who was studying the photograph said to the Ted holding the photograph, that was a long, long time ago, and the presence you had a long time ago was with your parents at church, and you are with them there now, a boy with your parents in church. They could not let you know how they were when they died, as if dying was their final and exclusive love for one another that you had not known about until their letters; their deaths so soon one after the other, it was as though they had wanted to die together in this bed.

He let the photograph fall onto the bed. He was tired. He had flown from London to Boston with only two days to sort out all the business of the inheritance, the clearing out and the selling of the apartment, which, for what it was worth, he would put in the hands of a lawyer and a real estate agent. He had a meeting back in London he must be at.

In a neighborhood restaurant, he took out his mobile from the inside pocket of his jacket to check if there were any messages for him on the little illuminated panel. He did this often, as if instinctively, but there was nothing urgent, and he paid for his meal and left. The trees alternated with electricity poles, the wires of which passed through the illuminated leaves into darkness.

The house was cold, and there was no hot water, and it seemed to him that the lights were dim.

He would sleep in his parents' bed because it was the only one made up by the doctor's wife.

In the dark, he held close to his eyes the photograph of himself on the Sunday of his Holy Communion. Yes, he remembered the prayer book, but that was all he remembered: it had a shiny black cover, and inside the front cover, as if in a shallow niche, was a small white crucifix with a golden Corpus. He put the photograph on the bedside table, and, undressing quickly to his underwear, he got into bed. The sheets were damp with cold, and he shivered a little, perhaps with more than the cold dampness.

He had been so unhappy in this house, where he had never, ever felt his parents were happy—never, as if the dark house did not allow happiness.

He sat up and switched on the bedside lamp. Shivering from the cold, he reached for the photograph again to study it in the light of the lamp.

There he was, in his white knee socks and white suit and white tie and his hair neatly combed and parted. He was, that boy, so far removed from Ted, he might have been any boy, not him, not Theodore Beauchemin. And he would put the photograph with the other mementos to be burnt in the backyard incinerator, for Ted heard Hilary telling him he was too sentimental, which he was.

He threw the photograph among the cards in the wastepaper basket and again switched off the light.

He was worried that he wouldn't be able to sleep. That was always a worry, because if he couldn't sleep, he knew that he wouldn't even be able to close his eyes against his thinking, but would lie awake and stare out into the dark of this dark house.

He would think of Hilary, of being at home with her, of being in London with her. She was there, and soon he'd be there with her, so when he did close his eyes, he could let go of the bed-

room where his parents had slept, sleeping in the
bed where his parents had died.

Let go, he said to himself. *Let go.*

Let go and think of Hilary, of being in bed
with her and her holding him.

Three

And how strange, he thought, that he was in an airplane hurtling through dark space.

Yes, he longed to be in London, though how could that be, how could London exist? How could the house he lived in there exist? How could Hilary exist, and their bed? Their bed, with soft sheets that often twisted about them when they made love, and, too, the pillows fallen to the floor when they made love.

Yes, yes, she would be in bed when he arrived, and he'd undress without waking her, waking her only when he raised the sheet to get into bed and take her in his arms. There would be the proof that Hilary existed, that their bed and house existed, and that London existed.

A very fine light began to show in the space outside.

She had given London to him, and, oh yes, he was happy there.

The space outside became more and more suffused with dawn, and there appeared a flame-colored tint to it, and then the sun rose.

And then Ted fell asleep.

In a dream there appeared a boy, ill and in bed, and Ted was standing by the bed, where he

gave the boy a small man in a gladiator's Roman
gear, which the boy took but then threw on the
floor where a gladiators' fight had occurred,
and in the midst of the fight the killed were,
one by one, dragged out of the arena by a horse,
leaving long ruts in the sand, to go into the unknown passages within the coliseum. They were
there, Ted and the boy, in a vast field where the
dead bodies of gladiators were skeletons in their
armor. And there were deep pits and fires and
many more dead bodies, some naked and some
with uniforms burnt away and revealing bleeding
muscles and wounds open to bones and skulls.
The boy asked, "Where are we? Why are there so
many dead? Tell me, I want to know."

Lights flicked on in the cabin, and he woke
when he was told to set his seat upright and fas-
ten his seat belt.

He was light-spirited. He could be light-spirited. It was in him to be, somewhere in him, and
in some way that spirit was finally released in
him because of Hilary.

And he thought, on the train into Paddington
Station, and in the taxi through London, here I
am, and it's fine, it's all good. And the sun was
now up and shining on pedestrians, on automo-
biles, on red double-decker busses, on London.

London, where he would live all the life he had left to live, which, given he was—what? thirty-seven—and Hilary just a little bit older, gave him years more to be able to say, This is London, this is my London . . .

And to let himself into the house, and to climb the stairs quietly, and to find the door to their bedroom open, and to find Hilary asleep on his side of the bed, and to undress so as not to wake her, and naked, to get into bed beside her, she naked, and, as if he had not been away but had been there all night in their bed, to feel her, awake or not, turn to fit her back against his chest, and for him to put an arm over her.

And to think, how safe I am here, how much in love.

Four

He so liked to lie in bed with her, liked to see the sunlight shining about the edges of the closed curtains creating a space in the dimness that had little to do with the room, a delicate space in which he and Hilary lay in their bed after they made love. The sheets over their naked bodies were loose and rumpled, and one of Hilary's legs was half wrapped in it, her exposed foot dangling over the edge of the mattress.

Ted turned sideways towards her and reached out to her to run the tips of his fingers across her forehead. He brushed the locks of hair that stuck to her forehead back to her temples. With his index extended from his large, big-knuckled hand, he traced her brow and nose, her lips, her chin, her jaw. His finger descended the side of her neck to a breast and he placed his hand over it. Hilary woke and yawned, a deep yawn.

Outside in the street, a child, free from school on this Saturday morning, called out, "Ted, Ted!" and ran past, below the window.

"Is he calling for you?" Hilary whispered.

He smiled and whispered back, "For some other Ted."

He had a broad, blond face, and his hair was receding and his forehead was high. His shoulders were big, and the white muscle of the arm extended towards her was large and just a little slack. He withdrew his hand from her breast and folded it with his other hand against his chest, and she put her arms about him. He fell asleep in her arms.

Slowly, so as not to wake him, she disengaged herself from him, and, his eyes closed, he held his head up and, with the soft, guttural sound of his tongue rising and pulling away from his palate, he opened and closed his lips, then his head fell to the pillow.

Barefoot, her dressing gown tied loosely about her, she went downstairs to the basement kitchen and out the back door into her garden to work there for an hour in the warm late morning sunlight. She had deliberately put it off because of what she'd known Ted wanted from her. She pulled up weeds before they flowered and their seeds spread and she dropped the weeds—dock, speedwell, chickweed, dandelion—into a green plastic bag, already bulging with wilting stalks and leaves from the day before, and she wondered why it seemed to her that Ted appeared more and more sad when they both had every reason to be

happy. The impulse came to her to go back to
him in their room.

Leaving the bag, her gardening gloves thrown
by it, she stepped from paving stone to paving
stone, her light dressing gown nudged about her
legs and thighs by the peonies, lupins, delphin-
iums, irises, marguerites, cornflowers among
which she moved. When she reached the doors of
the little greenhouse at the back of the house, she
turned to examine her garden.

She was concerned about the roses, the ram-
bling roses on a brick wall whose leaves seemed to
be eaten by insects, perhaps by wasps, she wasn't
sure.

She found that Ted was still asleep. Standing
above him, she didn't want to wake him, but
they'd be late for the garden luncheon party
they'd been invited to. She didn't mind not going, but he would.

She leaned close over him and said softly,
"Ted." This startled him awake. When he opened
his eyes and looked up at her, an expression in
them made her stand back and ask, "What's the
matter?"

He shook his head and laughed. Startled, she
too laughed. Ted lifted the sheet high, then drew
it down quickly so it billowed up and he, naked,
jumped out from beneath it and stood. He and

she watched the sheet, twisting as it fell, settle in a tangle on the bed.

Hilary said, "I wish we weren't going out so I could get back to my garden."

Tugging at his scrotum, Ted frowned. Hilary knew he always considered what she did and didn't want, so if she didn't want to go out he perhaps shouldn't want to either. He said, now in an American accent that he could bring up from before the ten years of living with her in England and assuming something of a soft-spoken accent of his own, "I was sort of looking forward to going to the party."

"To meet people?" she asked with a lilt. She was playing a little with him, which she knew he liked her to do. Yes, he liked to play.

He said, "And I'd quite like to see Jonathan."

She touched his cheek and said, "We'll go to the party."

"Not if you don't want to."

"No, I suddenly want to," she said, but she knew it would be difficult to convince him, because he was always aware of what she wanted to do as more compelling than he wanted. "Honestly. I'll continue weeding when we return."

But he stood before her, naked, tugging like a boy at his scrotum.

"Get dressed," she said.

As eager as Ted always was to go to a party, getting ready always took him a long time. Hilary, though she was always prompt, didn't much mind Ted taking his time. She returned to her garden to continue to pull out goosegrass, nettles, chickweed. By the time Ted came down to find her she had green stains on her long skirt.

"I'm sorry I took so long," he said.

"Don't be." She lifted her skirt where the stain was, examined it, and let it fall within a fold. "The later we get there, the sooner we can leave."

"You're going because of me."

"Reason enough."

The taxi took them through London, in which the early June sunlight sometimes entered the taxi and illuminated Ted's clear profile. He was pensive. Hilary asked, "Is something wrong?"

He turned to her with an expression of surprise on his bright, blond face and asked, "Why are you asking?"

"You seem sad."

"Well, sad about my parents."

"Yes, of course, and I am sorry."

She reached out and ruffled his hair.

He said, "It is better that they died."

"You say that as though there was nothing to save them."

"There wasn't."

"No one can be that hopeless."

"Well, they were."

"Then I needn't ask about them. I never did. I thought you didn't want me to."

He looked away from her, out the taxi window, where the light was so bright he closed his eyes. She leaned toward him and kissed his temple.

To her, he appeared to have come from a country she knew nothing about, born and brought up in a house in a town in a country that was his own, and there was constant dark in the country.

But here, she thought, here, she was able to bring him into her light, and she knew he knew this, he knew she loved him, and she did. She loved him, as now when she felt that he had withdrawn into that country she would bring him out of, by again pressing her lips to his temple and whispering, "You are my Ted."

"Am I?" he asked.

"Unless I meet another Ted."

"Like me?"

"Oh, much, much more Ted."

He turned his head to kiss her and smile.

The garden luncheon party was at Colin and
Jessica Kerr's house in St. John's Wood, in a large,
detached brick house with a gravel drive to the
front door and shadowed in this bright afternoon by high, leaf-heavy trees. As Ted was paying the taxi driver, Hilary, beside him, looked up
through the trees, their leaves dark green against
the shining pale sky.

She would have preferred getting right back
into the taxi and returning home to her garden
and her domestic life with Ted. These were all
she wanted, though her social connections in
London could have her and Ted out for lunches and dinners whenever he was free from work.
She often kept invitations from him because he
would have wanted her to accept them.

A tall woman, as tall as Ted, she was dressed,
as usual, loosely, with a long, beige blouse hanging over a longer, darker beige skirt, and a soft
scarf about her neck that reached below the hem
of her skirt and swayed with her slow, swaying
movements, her hands raised at the wrists and
held out. Her hair, thick, swung with her slow
movements.

The black taxi drove off and Ted remained
standing on the gravel looking at Hilary until she
took his arm to go to the door of the house. The
Filipino maid, Rosemary, opened the door, not

only to let Hilary and Ted in but to let out a couple first. The guests were leaving. Rosemary shut the door behind Hilary and Ted to go, not with them downstairs, but upstairs, as if she was needed by someone there. Ted followed Hilary to the end of a passage and down the stairs to another passage that led out, at the back of the house, to the garden with a great chestnut tree where the remaining guests were gathered in small groups.

Jessica, whose party this was, was standing with an elegant African man and woman, as though not sure what to talk about with them and not sure how to leave them. When she saw Hilary and Ted, she waved and, smiling a wide smile as if to her closest friends, she stepped away from the couple to greet them.

Five

Hilary felt the weight of her body among the guests at the garden party, but she allowed Ted the spirit he had of liking everyone by following him as he spoke to other guests or made spirited gestures to them on the way to where Jessica was standing under the large chestnut tree with an aged Black couple Hilary did not know.

Jessica kissed Ted, then Hilary, on their cheeks, then, with an apparent appeal to their helping her, she introduced them to the couple, he in a black, pinstriped suit and she in a simple black frock.

Ted looked about and exclaimed, "What a great day." Then he turned to Jessica and asked, "But where is Jonathan?"

"He's upstairs in bed in his room. Colin says he has a bit of flu, that's all. Colin's not very indulgent of illness."

"Rosemary is looking after him?"

"She puts us to shame, rather. She's given him a rosary to carry when he makes his Holy Communion."

"Jonathan's going to make his Holy Communion?"

"He's anxious that he won't be well enough."

Gesturing towards the couple, Jessica said to Hilary and Ted, "Mr. and Mrs. M'toko," and she added, as if to her this distinguished him as someone whom she would invite to a garden party, "Mr. and Mrs. M'toko are from Rhodesia."

Jessica knew nothing about British history, Hilary thought, and perhaps little about African history. Jessica lived in the history of her poetry.

Pinned to the large bosom of the woman was a brooch with diamonds.

Frowning, Hilary asked Mr. M'toko, "You say you are from Rhodesia?"

"That is where I was born and grew up and where I fought in the Rhodesian army, and now I say I am a Rhodesian veteran, even though it was a long time ago."

"You fought to keep Rhodesia a British colony?"

"I did, yes. And I became British."

"Don't be alarmed," Hilary said. "You can be as British as you want to be and then tell me what it is to be British."

Ted said to Jessica, "It's strange, but when I was in my parents' house, I found, in a metal box with legal documents, a photograph of myself the day I received Holy Communion."

"Strange," Jessica said.

Ted asked, "When does he make his Holy Communion?"

Frowning a little, she said, "He's supposed to tomorrow." Frowning more, she tried to place her husband somewhere in the midst of the party. "Where is Colin?"

"There," Ted said, "he's dead-heading that rose bush."

"Without secateurs, I see. Why we should have these parties when he acts as if no one were here, I don't know," Jessica said, and she crossed the lawn to say goodbye to departing guests.

Hilary stood silent with the African couple, as though the silence held back all of British and African history, and no one knew how to begin to talk about Rhodesia as a British colony and Zimbabwe as an African nation.

And Ted, as though there was nothing he could say to start the talk, except that he was against the crimes of colonization, of course he was, turned and walked away among the few guests. On his way, he all at once had the impression that everyone left at the party was standing still and that he was isolated in the stillness.

At his feet in the grass was a little figure of a naked man, abandoned there, and Ted reached down to hold it in his palm, this rigid plastic body with suggestive genitals, naked but for greaves and a breast plate and a helmet, the breast plate fitted close to the chest.

Approaching Colin, Ted held out on his palm the little soldier. "This must be Jonathan's."

Colin took it onto his own palm for the whole world to see it for a moment of silence.

He said, "I want Jonathan to be well educated, yes, I do, and to learn history, and so I approve of these little fantasies of history." He continued to study the little naked figure of a Roman soldier in his hand and he said, "If I am sometimes sharp with him, that is for discipline."

Ted asked, "What does that have to do with a Roman soldier?"

"Discipline," Colin answered. He handed back the Roman soldier to Ted and, looking about, he said, "Yes, discipline. It is how I have got through life."

Ted thought about Colin, that it was only because he was of gentry that he allowed himself to live what he imagined as a life of discipline. Really, Colin lacked discipline. He was known for that, and was even thought amusing because of it, as his suddenly turning away to deadhead roses by twisting them off at their stems, which even Ted knew a disciplined gardener did not do.

There was something—oh, what?—charming in Colin thinking he was the most disciplined person in the world. It was a wonder how he could keep up whatever discipline was needed to be taken seriously in the world he lived in—a world which he appeared to be unaware of when he held up a rose to study it for a long while and then made a gesture as if throwing the rose out into where dead roses go. Ted thought he heard Colin quote something in Latin.

In anyone else, Ted would have thought this was an intolerable pretension. It would have been an intolerable pretension in Ted if he tried it, which he wished he dared to do. But in Colin, it appeared to be his right, and Colin acted on his rights.

Ted asked, "What did you say?"

And Colin answered indifferently, "The rose, too, dies," and in that Colin struck Ted as a superior person and that was because Colin was a superior person.

He said, very simply, "The sorry history of humans is a game for boys," and he gave the Roman soldier back to Ted and turned away to twist another rose from its stem.

Ted put the dead Roman soldier into the side pocket of his jacket.

He said, "Jessica tells me that Jonathan is worried that he won't be able to make his Holy Communion tomorrow."

Colin laughed a little, vaguely, giving the impression that Jonathan's Holy Communion was not very important. But Ted knew Colin often laughed, a light laugh, whenever he was asked about something that Ted thought should have been important to him, and this light, vague laugh Ted never understood. He didn't understand why Colin seemed to be only vaguely present at his own party.

He said, "Jessica will make a fuss whenever Jonathan has a slight flu."

Colin plucked another wilted rose and dropped it, and Ted had the impression, behind his vagueness, of a person of his own private concerns. Not even being a host at a party in his own garden would bring him out of his private, thoughtful concerns.

A thin flat cirrus cloud, like a sheet, floated above. There were no other clouds.

Colin switched to another bush. Ted followed him and watched him, but for all that Ted wanted to ask him, Colin, he knew, wouldn't respond.

Looking up again, Ted saw that cirrus cloud fold in on itself and unfold and appear slowly to fall.

"Who are the African couple I abandoned Hilary to?"

"I don't know, Jessica invited them," Colin answered.

Jessica was striding towards them.

Colin said, "She will have these parties, inviting people for no reason I can think of, as I hardly know any of them, nor does she. I think it's American of her."

If Jessica heard, she reacted with a little command. "Colin, please behave and at least say goodbye to the guests."

Colin's eyes became a little out of focus as he crossed the lawn to guests waiting to say goodbye.

Ted said to Jessica, "I'd like to come to Jonathan's Holy Communion."

"Please do. Colin and I seem not to be up to it all when it means so much to the boy. It would mean a lot to him if you did come. Now I'd better say goodbye to the people Colin is meant to be saying goodbye to." She turned away, then turned back. "The ceremony will be at Mass in the Farm Street church."

"Thanks."

She again turned away.

Ted picked an overblown rose from a bush, dropped it, and picked another and let it fall to the ground.

He had supposed Holy Communion, with so much else, had ceased to exist in the Catholic Church.

Hilary came to him as he held out a rose, which she took, and asked, "Why did you leave me with the African couple? You said nothing and walked off."

Ted said, "Colin is sure that all Jonathan has is a little flu and that he will make his Holy Communion."

"What are you doing to that rose bush?"

"Dead-heading it, the way Colin did."

"Obviously, Colin knows nothing about gardening. And he has a terrible gardener. There's evidence of honey fungus everywhere, which means the whole of the garden should be dug up, the soil sterilized, and all new plants put in."

"You're eager to get back to your own," Ted said.

She touched his chin with the rose. "You're too good with people to be limited only to me. Go and talk to the African couple."

He said, "I don't approve of colonies."

"You wouldn't—just like you not to. Go and tell them that. I myself am going to the library where I know there are bound copies of old *Plantsmen*, and reading about gardens would give me almost more pleasure than you do in bed."

He laughed when she threw the rose at him, she laughing too, as though the rose had been meant to communicate something with him she was not sure he understood, but he liked the gesture. He was a person who was touched by gestures he had no understanding of beyond his catching the rose in his hands and holding it up to his face.

She left him, her long skirt swinging, and as she approached the house, she stopped to talk with Jessica. The two women laughed at something one of them said, and Ted had the vivid impression of a world they were connected to in London, Jessica through Colin's birthright, and Hilary through her own.

Jessica was a thin, short woman, angular, and her sharp face was made all the sharper by her hair, finely layered close to her head. She moved as if someone above her were always watching her for a lack of coordination, someone who would note—not criticize, for this was, among those who noted such matters, not criticism but merely observation—she, the American, was fitting herself into being the British Lady Kerr. She may at times have moved with slight jerks of her shoulders and arms, but she sustained, if somewhat stiffly, some elegance.

Compared to her, Hilary, who could not in-
herit the Commander of the British Empire given
to her father for his duty to the defunct British
Empire, had inherited an almost sloppy ease.

When Hilary went toward the house, Ted
went, not to the African couple who were still
standing alone, but to Jessica.

He said, "I'd like to see Jonathan."

A voice from the garden over the brick wall
called out, "Darling, darling."

Jessica insisted, "Please go see the African
couple."

"And ask them how they got that diamond
broach?"

"Well, one does wonder."

There was no response.

Ted asked, "May I go up to his room now?"

Jessica said, "Go on," as if she were giving up
on the party.

And she went to the African couple, who em-
phasized their delight for the delightful party.

Jessica did berate herself a little for having
invited them because they were rich, her social
fault; for all their thanking her, they clearly had
not had a delightful time, and Jessica wished she
had shown them more attention.

Six

Jonathan was in bed. The boy sat up in the midst of his duvet and took the little body Ted handed him and then dropped it on the floor, among other tiny men and women, dressed and undressed, spread out, the legs and arms of some interlocked as if in a heap of the dead. Jonathan closed his eyes for a moment and frowned, as though from pain, and when he opened his eyes, still frowning, he stared at Ted.

Ted kept his voice calm and low. "Your mum told me you're going to make your Holy Communion tomorrow."

"Even if I'm ill tomorrow, I'll go."

"Why do you have to, Jonathan?"

"I've just got to."

Jonathan fumbled in the folds of the duvet.

"What are you searching for?" Ted asked.

"For the rosary Rosemary gave me."

"I'll help you find it," Ted said, and he leaned to run his hands into the duvet until he came up with the rosary, which he gave to Jonathan, who held it stretched between his hands. The rosary was of white beads. The silver crucifix swung.

As absurd as it was—and the absurdity of it should have checked his feelings—Ted felt envious of Rosemary for having given the present to Jonathan.

The boy pressed the crucifix to his forehead.

Seven

The many panes of the large window of the library were bright, but the light did not penetrate the dim interior, painted dark green. In the library, there was not one object that did not conventionally belong there, including a large magnifying reading glass with a twisted antler as a handle on the green desk blotter. Hilary sat in a worn, deep leather sofa with a folded, tartan lap rug hanging over an arm, and she read the red buckram-bound volume of old copies of *The Plantsmen* she had taken from the floor-to-ceiling shelves of red and calf-brown books with gold lettering on the spines.

She sat up when Jessica came into the library, switched on the lamp with a green glass shade on the desk behind the sofa, and in the light raised a sheet of paper to read something on it, then placed it back on the desk and switched off the light and came round and sat next to Hilary.

"The last guest has gone," she said.

"Where I wonder is Ted?" Hilary asked.

"Speaking with Jonathan."

"I'll go and tell him we should leave."

"Let him speak with Jonathan. It always does the boy good when Ted speaks with him."

Hilary closed the book on her lap and shifted her weight a little, so the broken springs of the
sofa made the cushions slant at different angles
and the women were tilted towards each other.

The caterer, in street clothes, appeared at the
doorway. "Lady Kerr?" he asked.

"Yes?" Jessica responded.

"We've finished."

"And Colin isn't around to pay you. Who
knows where he is? Please come in." Jessica got up
and went to the desk behind the sofa and made
out a check, but again raised the sheet of paper
left by the lamp, and as she read, a little frown
occurred above her eyes, but she put the sheet of
paper down and brought the check to the caterer,
who had remained at the door.

Jessica again sat next to Hilary, both wom-
en angled toward each other, and Jessica said, "I
wonder if, married to Ted, as American as I suppose I am, I would understand him better than I
do Colin."

Hilary said, "You might give it a try with
him."

"Marrying him or understanding him?"

"Perhaps understanding him to start off with.
As for marrying him, we'll talk about that later." Hilary didn't want to go on about Ted. "He's
been with Jonathan a long time."

"Let him be," Jessica said.

As though she had been thinking about him, she said, "I try very much to understand him."

"What don't you understand?"

Hilary raised a hand as if to answer, or to avoid answering. Then she added, "Oh, he can seem to be trying to keep up his high spirits when he suddenly can't any longer and I feel he doesn't have the strength to keep them up."

"Is he so weak?"

"In some ways, yes, in some ways. And I do my best to keep his spirits up by telling him he has no reason not to, and that does help, for a while."

"Until?"

"Oh, until I feel I should again tell him he has no reason not to keep his spirits up, and he listens."

"He has you."

"He has me," Hilary said calmly. "Well, I'll go and tell him we must leave."

Not Hilary, but Jessica rose from the sofa and walked round to the desk, where, once again, she picked up the sheet of paper, read, and dropped it.

Hilary, too, rose. "I really should go find Ted and go with him now," she said.

Jessica only said, "Oh, I don't know."

"What don't you know?"

"About everything."

Hilary said, "I really must go."

"Then you go and leave Ted here."

But she wouldn't leave without Ted.

"I'm sure he has work to do," she said, and, without saying more, she left the library into the hall and climbed the stairs.

The house was so silent it might have been empty. It was only when she was near the doorway to Jonathan's room that she heard a voice and she stopped.

She heard Ted ask, "What do you pray for?"

A boy's clear, sexless voice answered, "For everyone."

"Everyone?"

"Yes, everyone in the world."

"And what do you pray for when you pray for everyone?"

"That everyone will love one another."

"Do you believe that's possible?"

"If everyone loved God it would be."

Hilary, leaning against the wall, heard nothing more, and she was about to enter the room when Ted spoke, and what he said startled her and made her go very still.

"Will you pray for me?"

"I'll pray for you."

In the silence, she remained where she was, then she walked quietly back down the passage and halfway down the stairs, as confused by what she had heard as if she had heard something she shouldn't have, something that she was sure Ted would not have wanted her or anyone to hear. Pausing on the stairs, her hand on the banister to steady herself, she turned round and called in a loud voice, "Ted."

He came to the top of the stairs.

She said, "We really should go," as though she had to keep her distance from Ted and Jonathan together.

"Come in and say hello to him."

She couldn't say no, and, passing Ted to go along to Jonathan's room, what she saw first as she entered the room was the window, and through the window, dark against the afternoon light, the great chestnut tree in the back garden.

When Ted turned to Hilary, she saw tears in his eyes.

More alarmed, Hilary on her way out couldn't make herself say goodbye to Jonathan, but, in her forward thrust to get out of the room as quickly as possible, she hit her shoulder against the doorjamb.

Going downstairs with her, Ted asked, "He will be all right, won't he?"

"Of course he will be. Now wipe your tears away."

He did, with the palms of his hands.

They let Rosemary pass by to go up to Jonathan.

Jessica was waiting for them in the library, greenish in the light of the brass lamp with a green glass shade on the desk. "How did you find him?" she asked.

Ted said, "He told me he finds it difficult to move his head because his neck is stiff."

"That doesn't sound good to me at all."

Then Colin, as though he had been wandering about the house, came in.

"Where have you been?" Jessica asked him.

In reply, he laughed a vague laugh.

"Ted tells me that Jonathan now has a stiff neck."

"Because he's been lying in bed too long."

About to ask if, at least, Jonathan's temperature had been taken, Hilary thought she mustn't interfere, and she said, "Ted and I must go."

"Please stay," Jessica said.

"No, I must get us home."

She didn't look at Ted, whose eyes, she thought, must have been red, Jessica and Colin wondering why they were, perhaps thinking something had happened between him and Hilary.

Out in the street, waiting for a taxi to come along, Ted asked Hilary, "Why didn't you even say goodbye to Jonathan?"

She tried to control her voice by raising the pitch. "For heaven's sake, he's only a boy and not to be made a great fuss over. You're making too much of a fuss over him."

Ted walked out into the street to look down it. A taxi was coming along.

Sitting together in the back seat, Hilary, who had little tolerance for awkward silences and none at all now, said, "I think Jessica has those garden parties only because she imagines they expand her social circle beyond Colin's small, boring circle." But as soon as she said this she regretted it not only because she had no reason to say it, but because Ted would wonder what possible reason she could have had for saying it. She corrected herself by adding, "Though perhaps she's simply interested in meeting people. I think that's very American, always wanting to meet people. Isn't it?"

"I like to meet people," Ted answered.

The taxi was in the midst of traffic around Hyde Park Corner, there where, from the top of the grand Constitution Triumphal Arch, the bronze statue of Victory, with large wings and holding high a laurel wreath, rode her chariot, pulled by four rearing horses in the reins of a boy, up into the blue sky.

Eight

Ted said he would go up to his desk, and Hilary returned to her garden, the best place for her to think.

She pulled out a weed, or she thought it was a weed, but examining it, she wasn't sure, and wished she hadn't uprooted it.

There were moments when Ted would suddenly hug Hilary closely and half shout what a lucky man he was to be married to her! But then he would let her go and turn away and, frowning, look out a window and say he hadn't known that it was raining out, the rain now all he was attentive to. He could welcome friends for a dinner party she had arranged—always her friends, for Ted seemed not to have friends of his own, seemed to count on her for her friends, who were, she thought, people he probably wouldn't have met on his own, from a world that was not his. But after drinks in the sitting room and at the table in dining room, the dinner served by an old woman Hilary said had been a domestic help to her parents, Ted would become silent, and she'd be left to raise the conversation by talking about other friends and then excuse herself to Ted by telling him he hadn't met them, but she'd make sure he did, and he would sit up and smile and say, "That would be great."

What was the difference between a garden plant and a weed? she asked herself.

And it did happen that he would get out of bed after their Saturday afternoon of love and go out because there was something more import-ant to him that pulled at him. She had never sus-pected that what was wrong with him and pulled at him was something that needed prayer to be made right.

The difference might be the flowers, she thought, though so-called weeds could produce beautiful, delicate flowers.

Hilary would not admit this, but she felt that Americans were more—what?—shadowed than the British, and it was that, that sense in them of the shadows against her clarity, that made her wonder about Ted, and about Jessica, too, both being Americans, though that they both were American seemed to be of no interest to either of them.

Hilary was not interested in people from be-fore she met them, as though their lives began when she met them, and that meant, especially, Ted.

She thought, his parents had died, and she must understand that about him; that was

enough for him to ask to be prayed for, to weep.
He had to think she was unfeeling, which she
wasn't, no, she wasn't.

She stood from digging and knocked earth
from the trowel, then, as if all at once aware, she
studied the shadows in the now sunless garden,
and she thought of how shadows in a garden were
in themselves a different garden, one to walk
about.

She should go in to tell Ted that they would
prepare supper together.

But she wandered among the shadows of the
garden.

Ted had talked with the boy as a way of helping the boy in his illness, a way of engaging with
him for the boy to feel some reassurance in be-
liefs that Ted himself perhaps still had. Perhaps,
Hilary thought, because she hadn't ever asked
Ted about his being a Catholic. Having little interest in any religion, she wasn't much interested if Ted was a believer in his. As she thought,
she gathered a bouquet of lilacs, snapping the
branches.

He came out to her to say he had laid the table in the kitchen for supper, and he exclaimed
such pleasure at the sight of her with the large
bunch of lilacs in her arms, and when a branch
fell to the gravel, he rushed to pick it up, and it

pleased her to see him hold out to her the branch with purple blossoms and large, dark leaves.

They were always holding out flowers to each other.

Ted was always, she thought, on the edge of being something of a parody of himself.

He lay the lilacs on the table and he looked at her as if to ask if that was all right of him to do.

She had such tenderness for him.

And they took pleasure in their simple lunch down in the kitchen, the door to the garden open to the damp freshness from outside, and the scents.

She so loved the way he stood after their meal and, yawning, stretched out his arms wide, as though even in that way he took pleasure in his body. And for her own pleasure she stood and pressed a hand to his warm chest, moist because the night was hot.

"Don't leave me now," she said.

"Only if we go out into the garden together."

They sat where roses grew on a trellis.

She said, "I would like to help you to put an end to your grief."

"Is it grief? I don't know what it is."

"Something," she said.

"Yes, something. I don't know what. They seemed to want to die."

"Planned by them?"

"I don't know. There was something of a service in the funeral parlor and the burial, and there were so few people I left and went to the house to spend the night before leaving the next morning. I slept in their bed."

"No, Ted, no."

"The doctor's wife had remade it for me. Their bedroom was the only warm room in the house."

"I'm sorry that that's the last you'll think of them."

"I found out that they had been away from each other for a long enough time that they wrote letters to each other, and, you know, when they did come back together again, I was born. And here I am."

"Here you are."

Nine

Jessica lay awake next to Colin, who was snoring lightly, his facial muscles sometimes twitching.

Colin's refusal to make what he called a fuss had often been his reassuring advice to her—let it be, it will sort itself out—and often he'd been right.

Jessica was shocked, sometimes, by how strong his will was, as when he found that Jonathan was being uncivil, or just stupid, and he'd reprimand him severely. But the flash of will lasted only a moment, just long enough for Jonathan to learn the lesson, though Jessica did not like his flicking a finger sharply against Jonathan's skull.

Colin stopped snoring, and Jessica could hardly hear him breathing.

She got up in the dawn light to go to their son's room. Jonathan had come late in their married lives. The duvet disordered as if he had thrashed in it, he lay awake, and in a weak voice he said that he felt hotter, that his headache was worse, and that he couldn't move his head.

"Why didn't you come to us?" Jessica asked.

"I kept waiting for it to go away."

Jessica quickly returned to Colin and woke him by touching his shoulder. Colin never seemed to sleep deeply, his eyelids half open, and sometimes wide open. Yet if Jessica woke him, he jolted and sat up with an expression of having been so deeply asleep he had no idea where he was, or who woke him. His bald head was white, the strands of hair usually combed over it falling over an ear, and his eyes were round in round, dark sockets.

Jessica said, "Jonathan is worse," and he threw back the bed covers, and without putting on his dressing gown over his too-small pajamas, hurried out, saying sharply, "I'll deal with this," as if he were going to reprimand Jonathan for being worse.

But when, turning, she saw him standing in the doorway as if unable to make himself enter, she asked, "What shall we do?"

He combed his hair over his pate with his fingers.

She pushed past him and out to a little study off the landing, used by her mainly to make telephone calls, and in an address book, blue leather stamped with gold stars, she looked up the emergency number of their doctor, Dr. Herbert, and rang.

Waiting for Dr. Herbert to arrive on this early Sunday morning, Jessica sat by her son's bed, holding his hand as he lay, with a frown of pain, his eyes closed. Colin, still unable to make himself enter, remained at the doorway.

He didn't move when the door knocker sounded throughout the house. Jessica rushed past him to let Dr. Herbert in. Colin was not waiting at the top of the stairs. Only after Dr. Herbert had examined Jonathan, Jessica standing by him, did Colin, as if he had alone been wandering about the house, appear at the doorway to the room, but he didn't enter.

Jonathan was wrapped in the duvet by Jessica, who in her nightgown and dressing gown, carried him bundled downstairs and out to the car parked in the drive. Colin, he too in his dressing gown, followed. Dr. Herbert said that they must all get into his car. In the back seat, Jessica cradled the long, lanky body of their son wrapped in the duvet.

Sunday morning, London in the early sunlight was as still as if its inhabitants were shut up in their homes and waiting for an enemy invasion.

In the entrance lobby of the hospital in Devonshire Place, Jonathan was taken from Jessica's arms, and, her arms still extended, she turned to Colin, but, unshaven, the strands of his hair falling crookedly over his bald head, he turned away.

In his slippers, his ankles and heels exposed, Colin paced the passage outside Jonathan's room, and Jessica leaned against a wall of the passage and looked down, below the hem of her dressing gown, at the tips of her red slippers with red satin bows.

Colin turned away and pressed his forehead against a wall.

After a long while, during which people—another doctor and hospital staff—entered and left Jonathan's room, Dr. Herbert came out and gently took Colin and Jessica aside to tell them that Jonathan had infectious meningitis, but that everything was being done for his recovery.

The boy lay with a drip hanging by the bed, the tube ending in a needle inserted in the back of his hand and held with tape, his hand placed over his chest. He tried to sit up when he saw his parents come into the room, but he fell back, frowning.

He said, angry at them, "I've got to make my Holy Communion."

"You'll make it," Jessica said, quickly going to the bed. "You'll see, we'll arrange for you to make it another time, soon. What is the name of the priest who has been instructing you, darling?"

"Father Ridge."

"Your papa will speak to Father Ridge."

Jonathan frowned more angrily. "I want to make it now."

"You will soon, darling, you will," Jessica said. "Colin, tell him you'll speak to Father Ridge. Tell him."

"I will," Colin said.

Jonathan was frowning the way his father did when, all at once intolerant of someone's lack of consideration, he said to his mother, "But aren't you going to receive Communion?"

"Without you?" Jessica asked.

Unlike his father but like his mother, Jonathan's outraged feelings didn't last for only a moment, but were long lasting, even relentless. And unlike his father and like his mother, his feelings quickly led him to being irrational, and he insisted, "You've got to go."

Jessica called, "Colin."

"Of course we'll go," Colin said.

"You may be too late, and it'll all be over," the boy said.

"We'll hurry," Jessica said.

"Hurry, hurry."

"We'll go home and change quickly and go."

"Hurry!" Jonathan was shouting at them.

"We're going," Jessica said and embraced and kissed her son on his hot, damp cheek. "We're going." She found herself pushing at Colin, and she said to him, as angrily as had her son, "Hurry," and pushed past him, and he followed.

But in the hospital lobby he said, tapping his chest and thighs with his palms, "I have no money to pay for a taxi."

A rage passed through Jessica. "What has happened to you?"

"I left home without money," he said flatly.

She had to ask the receptionist to lend her ten pounds, and it was Jessica who, out into Devonshire Place in her slippers and dressing gown, hailed a taxi.

At home, she kept telling Colin to hurry. They dressed without bathing, he without shaving, she without makeup.

Colin drove round Mayfair trying to find a place to park until Jessica said, "Park illegally, park anywhere," and Colin, who would normally have protested, parked in an empty space with a double yellow line.

From outside the church, she heard the organ, and when Colin opened the door for Jessica and she saw the congregation and, beyond the heads, the blue and red stained-glass window above the altar and, below, the priest at the altar, she thought she should have called Ted to let him know that Jonathan wouldn't be making his first Holy Communion. Ted, and perhaps Hilary, were likely to be in the church. She couldn't see them. Not to make a disturbance, Colin indicated an empty back pew in a side aisle.

In the pew, Jessica once again tried to see if Ted was in the church. The line of pillars along the nave blocked her view of the altar except in narrow sections through which the priest appeared and disappeared. She looked up and to the side at statues of saints in Gothic niches, then looked down, directly to her left, at a side altar with a marble bas-relief of the Annunciation, which she both saw and didn't see. Then she looked further down to where, inserted into a niche below the altar, there was a matte white marble statue of a reclining figure, and the second her eyes met the figure a shock through her made her focus with so much attention it seemed to her that what she saw came up close to her. The statue was of a boy lying with pillows under his head, covered from the waist down by a blanket from which his naked feet protruded. Under an arm he held lilies, and in a hand, he clutched a rosary of large, round, white beads. He was looking directly at Jessica. The boy was dying.

Jessica left the pew to go to the statue under the side altar, aware of nothing else. It appeared to enlarge the way the boy's shirt was open at the neck, the way one bare foot was turned.

She heard a little bell ring, and she turned to the nave, where the congregation were kneeling for the elevation and consecration of the host, and she saw Ted and Hilary among them in the midst of people kneeling. In the pew she had left, Colin was kneeling, his head bent forward.

Jessica looked back, terrified, at the statue of the boy, and, above, to the words cut into the marble altar, *ad aeterna* on one side of a tabernacle with a golden door and *non caduca* on the other side. She did not understand.

Only when she became aware of movement in the church did she turn round once more to the nave. The children had made their Holy Communion. The organ was playing music that was meant to be joyful but echoed with some deeper, darker music. The congregation were leaving the pews to go to the front of the church to take communion themselves. Colin left the pew to join those in the main aisle who were lined up. Jessica returned to the pew and sat, unable to follow Colin.

She saw that Hilary and Ted were sitting alone in the pew, everyone else having left to go to the altar to receive. Ted grasped with one extended hand the back of the pew before him and pulled himself up, as if against the weight of his body, and passed Hilary to go along the empty pew to the end, where he remained and watched the communicants lined up in the aisle. He waited, it seemed, to be the last of them, but the last passed him and Ted didn't leave the pew, didn't join the line, as if waiting. Now Colin returned and knelt beside Jessica and lowered his face into his hands. She continued to watch Ted, who took a step out into the aisle, then took a step back and turned round and back to Hilary and sat motionless next to her.

At the end of the Mass, the children, five girls in white veils, processed down the main aisle while the congregation, standing, watched them pass. Jonathan would have been the only boy.

Reprimanding him, Jessica said to Colin, "Go tell the priest about Jonathan," and only then did he press his way among the exiting congregation to the other side of the church and down the side aisle to the sacristy.

She went out into the street, where the small girls in white veils mingled in the crowd. Some of the girls carried prayer books held up in both hands, from which dangled white ribbons affixed with white flowers. Jessica stood on the other side of the street to wait not so much for Colin as for Ted, who came to her ahead of Hilary. He asked, "Where's Jonathan? Why isn't he here?"

Ten

After Sunday lunch with Hilary, Ted left to go off to the bank in the city, as he often did at unexpected hours, even on a Sunday. When he returned, Hilary was again working in her garden, where Ted stepped into the circle made of a coiled garden hose.

He said, "I've got to go off to Helsinki right away for a meeting early tomorrow morning."

"I was looking forward to the evening with you."

"But what would we do if I lost my job?"

"You'd find another."

"You make it sound so easy."

She laughed. "Why shouldn't it be?"

Ted laughed, too, then stepped back out of the green, coiled garden hose and left to pack. She went up to the sitting room, where she felt more and more the time approaching when he must come down with his suitcase and say good-bye. Usually, she accepted this moment as one that occurred matter-of-factly in their daily lives, but now, when he did come down, she grabbed his shirt front as if to keep him from going.

His face appeared smoothed by the shadows in the room, and from within those shadows he said, "The car may be waiting."

She let him go.

But, instead of turning away, he waited as if for her to grab him again to keep him from going.

Then he said, "I'll just telephone Jessica to ask how Jonathan is."

"You have time for that?"

"It'll only take a minute."

He hurried into his study, off the sitting room, and she heard him speak. Coming back to her, he said, "Colin said he's slept and is better. Jessica's with him."

"I told you he would be better."

"I should always listen to you."

At the window, where the striped, faded curtains hung in swags with unraveling tassels to hold them back, Hilary, looking out, said, "Your car is here."

The walls of the narrow entrance hall were covered, the frames almost touching, with antique maps of the places Ted had traveled to for his work, and some were from before the discovery of America, with sea monsters out in the spaces beyond the known world. At the door, Ted embraced Hilary and kissed her forehead, then, as if after a quick shift in all his feelings, kissed her with the intensity of someone going far for a very long time, and Hilary responded to the intensity. She couldn't let him go, and now, kissing him again and again, she felt rise between them the arousal that always came with his leaving.

She said softly into his ear, "I want to tell you, don't go, don't go."

"All you'd have to do is say the word."

"Really?" she asked. "Really, all I'd have to do is say the word and you wouldn't go?"

"It would mean losing my job, but why should having a job be so important? So try me."

She pulled back from the impulse and pushed at Ted's shoulders. "Go on now. What would happen to us if you lost your work?"

He picked up his suitcase. "You'd find me another."

She opened the front door, and, holding it, she watched him get into the waiting car, wave through the window that was too bright for her to see more than a hand, and be driven off.

Alone, she went out to her garden, where, as if this were the reason why she came, she studied the irises.

The flowers were there, and she was there among the flowers, but neither she nor the flowers were quite there, and this made her very attentive to one iris, purple-black.

It was not in Hilary to say her garden was beautiful. She was not a person for words, and even to say that she expressed her feelings in flowers was to give the flowers too much meaning. She never thought of what anything meant, or not much. Her awareness was bright, but if there was some meaning in being aware, she had no idea what that could be. She concentrated on the convoluted iris, this iris.

Really, she was thinking about Ted.

She needed Ted. She found his expressions of wonder naïve, but from time to time she recognized in his sense of wonder her own, from when she was a girl in India reading English poetry and longing for rainbows arching from one green hill to another, for skylarks, for hedgerows of blossoming hawthorn, for still, vast lakes in the morning mist, and for a large garden. And now, now, she was filled with the wonder of her need for Ted, and wonder was to her a great and fulfilling awareness of the garden, of the house, of London, of his warm bodily presence in his absence.

When she turned to go into the house, there occurred to her such a wonderful moment of the awareness of Ted that she leaned for a moment against the brick wall next to the open doorway.

I love Ted, she thought. I do love him.

The moment of awareness remained with her, there where she was, a moment that came to her as if from a recollection from so deep in the past it might not have happened in fact. But it had happened, and would happen again when Ted returned, or so she had to believe, though how could she believe in something that might not happen again? Every time he left, the feeling came to her that he might not return. No, he would, of course he would, and she would have him again, and that was everything to her, that she would be in his arms. She was not original, she was even banal, but that didn't matter to her, because what mattered was to be in his arms, he gently kissing her face all over, again and again and again. When she was a girl, she imagined she was so grown up and experienced that someone like Ted was already a past memory, and now, an experienced woman, she did have the memory, and whatever happened, she would always have that.

She looked back at her garden, where the sunlight cast shadows among the flowers.

Eleven

In the half-empty first class section of the airplane, Ted sat apart from the other members of his team to study the analyst's report for the meeting in Helsinki. He wanted to be on his own. This was unlike him. Or maybe it was deeply like him, and it was in fact in Ted's character always to want to be on his own, a trait he countered, because he thought it wrong, by being overly friendly.

The review open on his lap, he was unable to sit still.

All his life he had had to fight against wishing he were someplace else, wishing he were someone else.

He walked up and down the first class aisle of the quiet airplane, in which the other members of his team were, themselves, sitting separately. The airplane tilted in odd directions and made him lose balance. Ted stopped at the seat of a member of his team to talk because he thought it unfriendly to pass by without some word, but he soon returned to his seat and, putting the analyst's report on his lap, looked out the window at a level of cloud that reached to the curving horizon. He could have been anywhere over the globe of the earth. The airplane kept titling slowly in odd directions.

He felt he was suddenly falling when there came to him the thought, Jonathan is going to die. And the sensation of falling made him sit up and look out the window at the clouds below the descending airplane.

He picked up the analyst's report from his lap and he forced himself to read it.

On his return from Helsinki in the taxi from the airport into London, Ted slid open the glass partition that separated him from the driver and said he had changed his mind about where he wanted to be taken. At the hospital reception, he was told that Lady Kerr was with her son, and Ted asked the receptionist to connect him with her by telephone. Jessica, in a voice that rose from a dull "hello" to a bright "Ted," told him to come up. The receptionist agreed that he could leave his bag with her, and feeling, himself, suddenly bright, he took the lift up to Jonathan's room.

Jessica met him at the door, her delicate face he saw flushed with the pleasure of seeing him.

"I came straight from the airport," he said.

"Does Hilary know?"

"No."

Jessica took Ted's hand to lead him to the side of the bed, where the sleeping boy looked thinner, paler, as if the pumping of his blood had abated with the abating of his fever.

"He's going to be well," she whispered.

Ted put his arm across Jessica's shoulders to press her to his side and then he let her go. She sat on a chair.

"Father Ridge will come here tomorrow to give Jonathan his First Communion," Jessica said. "Jonathan is very happy, so happy that I honestly think his happiness itself at receiving will make him better."

"I'm glad, I'm really glad."

"He asked me if you were at the ceremony, and I said yes."

"Did he ask if I received?"

"He did."

"What did you tell him?"

"I told him you did. I told him I did. Was that wrong?"

"Not if it helps him."

"I'd never before seen Colin receive." Jessica held her breath a moment, then shook her head and said, "I don't know why, but I couldn't. Why didn't you?"

"I couldn't."

Jessica nodded. "It wasn't because I wasn't prepared," she said. "It wasn't even that I'm not practicing, or even that I'm a sinner, or even that

I don't believe. Why I didn't, I think now, was because it was too much for me, all too much, and I couldn't comprehend anything of it, and I was terrified of my incomprehension. Has that ever happened to you? Has—"

But Jessica stopped and turned quickly to the bed, where Jonathan, raised on his elbows, said, "Mummy." She jumped up and leaned over him, but he didn't follow her with his eyes, which continued to stare out. "Mummy," he said again.

She leaned over him, saying, "Darling," but, though he did raise his eyes toward her, he seemed to look through her, and not seeing her, to call again, louder, "Mummy."

"I'm here, darling."

Jonathan didn't see her, didn't hear her, and, his voice raised in horror, he cried, "Mummy, mummy!" And his face contorted.

She put her arms about him and lifted him. His body was rigid except for the hand with the tube of the drip inserted into it that dangled. She said, "I'm here, darling."

"Don't let it in," the boy screamed.

A nurse came into the room, a Black nurse in a white uniform, and she said quietly, "He is delirious."

"Can't anything be done to stop the delirium?" Jessica pleaded.

The nurse, biting her lower lip, left the room.

The boy screamed, "It's coming in, Mummy, it's opening the door and coming in."

Jessica drew the boy closer to her, pressing his chest against her bosom, and she cried, "I won't let it in, darling, I won't let it in."

"It's opening the door, Mummy."

"I'll make it go away, darling, I'll make it go away." She rocked his body in her arms. "I'll make it go away, and we'll open the door wide and you'll see it's gone, it's gone and it won't come back." Jonathan closed his eyes, and Jessica shouted, to rouse him, "Look, look, darling, you see, I've opened the door all the way, and it's gone, it's gone."

Twelve

A strange longing came to Ted walking along Bond Street with his overnight case.

He thought that the longing was so deeply inculcated within him from when he believed that to live was to long to die, because to die was to live in eternity. That was the meaning of life, and though he did not believe that, the longing remained without knowing what now the longing was for, but it was in him, it was powerful in him.

The house appeared to Ted to be strange with the wonder of how it had happened that he was living there, the wonder of his living there with Hilary. It was strange that he was in London, in London where Chelsea and Belgravia merged, in what he had learned from Hilary to call a terrace house with columns on either side of the front door and a pediment above and a black iron fence before a sunken area.

He left his case in the hall and went into the drawing room—as he had learned from her to call it instead of the living room—and looked at the heavy, striped curtains and striped wall-paper and Oriental rugs on wall-to-wall carpet. On the chimneypiece—which he had called the mantlepiece but had learned to call chimneypiece from Hilary—was a stone head of Buddha, from India, the nose and cheeks chipped, the top and the back of the head reflected in a tilted mirror hung behind it. Facing the fireplace was a big sofa with pillows of Indian silk, on either side of which were armchairs also with pillows of Indian silk, and before the sofa was a large ottoman.

As if he had just arrived and was a visitor in a house when the proprietor had not yet turned up to meet him, he looked behind the folded screen by the door as if unsure what would be there, though he knew, of course he knew. The screen was pasted with cut-out Victorian oleographs of flowers and birds and children, and half hidden by the screen was a butler's tray on a stand with a yellow teapot and yellow-and-white teacups and saucers, all from India, where Hilary's father had been the head of the Old Chartered Bank of Australia, China, and India in Flora Fountain, Bombay, where Hilary was born and grew up. The house had not been changed or added to since their return to London and their deaths.

He went up to the bedroom with the case and took off his jacket and tie, and went to look for Hilary, he thought, in the garden.

She was not in the garden, nor back in the house sitting room reading a gardening magazine. He was not supposed to worry about where she was, but he became restless, wondering, after all, where Hilary was. Then it occurred to him that every Saturday morning she went to Clapham to do voluntary work in the garden of the hospice, and he decided to go and find her there. From Lower Sloane Street, he took a bus up to Clapham Common.

He pushed open a door at the back of the foyer of the large Georgian mansion into a large garden with benches in the shade of trees and a pond with reeds and ducks. He walked along a path between parterres of blue, white, yellow, and purple irises, and stopped when, in the distance, he saw Hilary, a rake held upright in one hand, sitting on a bench with a young man, listening to him. Talking, the young man slouched.

Hilary saw Ted and made a gesture he interpreted as a plea for him to stay away while the young man talked. But the young man noted the gesture, and though it was evident to Ted that Hilary asked him to stay, the young man got up and, nodding to her, turned and walked away, towards Ted. His clothes were wrinkled, soiled too, as if he'd worn them for days, and on his tender face was the soft stubble of an unshaven beard. He passed Ted without looking at him.

Hilary, in gumboots and gloves, was now raking the path of leaves.

He said, "I'm sorry, I interrupted."

"His grandpa just died," Hilary said, "and he wanted to talk."

"Does it happen often that people come out into the garden from the hospice and talk to you?"

"Sometimes. I never go into the rooms myself. There's not much I can do for them except to help keep up the garden. They look at it from their windows, or, if they're able to manage, they come out and walk along the paths or sit on a bench. They too get on somehow."

"Can I help you?" Ted asked.

"Yes, by raking the leaves from the path," she answered and pushed the rake handle towards him, so he took it.

She pruned a bush.

Though this disappointed him a little, he accepted her as she now was, but it did occur to him that there was nothing mysterious about Hilary, nothing. He wondered, as soon as this thought came to him, if it came as more than an observation, but as a judgment of something she lacked.

She came to him, moving slowly, and said she had some lunch they could share, and he followed her into a little trellised arbor over which jasmine grew.

He asked, "Doesn't it upset you that this is a place where people come to die?"

"I concentrate on making the garden as lovely as possible for them," she answered, smiling.

"You can do that, not allow your feelings to get involved, and yet be so kind, so generous, so attentive. I don't think I could—I mean, not allow my feelings to get involved."

"No," she said, "you couldn't."

"Is that wrong?"

"Wrong? No, no. It's what makes you you."

"I should be more like you."

"I'd hate it if you were like me," she said.

He laughed a light laugh and said, "I stopped first to see Jonathan in the hospital."

"How is he?"

"He'll be all right."

"Were Colin and Jessica there?"

"Jessica was."

"You left her alone."

"Yes."

"You should have stayed with her."

Ted simply shook his head, which might have meant he hadn't known what to do.

She said, "I had the odd feeling, when you left, that you wouldn't come back."

"Not come back? What could have happened to me that I wouldn't come back?"

"You go so often on long trips, and I thought it's all too possible that one day, for some reason I don't even want to consider, you wouldn't return."

"No, no," Ted said, "I would always return, no matter what happened to me."

"I was, I don't know why, especially lonely after you left."

"No longer, I hope."

She smiled a light smile. "No, no longer."

There, in the little arbor, Ted kissed her lips, her chin, her cheeks, her eyes, her forehead, over and over.

Hilary laughed a little and, as if the question were relevant to them now, she asked, "The meeting went well?"

"No, the meeting didn't go well."

"Then," she said, "we'll do something lovely to make up for that."

"What?" he asked.

"Well, first we'll have lunch out, and then, back home, we'll see."

Ted tried to smile, and Hilary knew he did this for her, in his appreciation of her for trying to raise his spirits, which were low. But there was a subtle sensuality in his lowered spirits, as if something there, in those low spirits, stirred. Hilary felt this in him, and she thought that to help him, as she wanted to do, it wouldn't be by mildly joking with him, but by allowing him whatever was stirring in him. Something in his sadness.

At a simple restaurant in Clapham, he said, "I stopped at the hospital to see Jonathan, but left when Jessica asked me to. Jonathan was delirious and his mother wanted to be alone with him to reassure him."

"What was he delirious about?"

"Something was coming into the room to take him away."

Hilary, understanding, simply said, "Yes."

He repeated, "Yes."

They walked to Clapham Village and at the bus terminal ascended to the top of the double-decker bus that was already waiting, both of them silent all the while. The bus started. They were the only passengers on the top, sitting together at the front, the window before them wide on the view below of small, grim cottages on either side. Ted raised an arm and placed it across the shoulders of Hilary, who sensed her tense shoulders give way under the weight of his arm, and she felt comforted. And yet, there was something in the comfort that made her wonder a little—made her wonder about Ted, who was there beside her, his body pressed against hers.

They went up to their bedroom, where Ted, heavy with all that he was feeling, lay on the bed dressed, and Hilary pulled off his shoes, then, also dressed, lay beside him.

He turned to her and kissed her, and she unbuttoned his shirt.

Tender as he was, there was, too, an awareness in his making love to her, a considerate, an almost intelligent awareness, that made the tenderness considerate, made it almost intelligent, when he drew back to look at her, to look at every part of her body with, she thought, wonder. The deepest reason for making love, deep, deep, deeper than the moist and smooth and soft but firm contacts of skin, was to make love roused by—

He said, "Oh my darling, oh my darling, oh my darling."

They slept, and when Hilary woke she found that she and Ted were tangled in a sheet, and a pillow was on the floor. She gently untangled the sheet from herself and sidled out of the bed, picked up the pillow and replaced it, and then stood back to look at Ted, still wrapped in the sheet.

When in her bath the scented steam rose about her, and she thought there was nothing in her life that merited the love she had in Ted. And she felt she had been touched by a love that had to be wayward for her to feel it, because how could love be so open to her, love she even withdrew a little from as though the openness made her vulnerable? It wasn't in her, that openness to love, but touched in her by Ted.

He couldn't help himself; he was the person he was. Of course Hilary believed one could help oneself.

When she was a child, if one didn't behave properly, one was sent up to one's room and told not to come down until one did behave properly.

Naked, just woken, Ted came into the bathroom.

He said, "I've just spoken to Colin. He said that Jessica is still with Jonathan, that she spoke and spoke with him, never stopped, and he woke up from his coma, woke up and recognized his mother."

"Colin told you?"

"You don't believe him?"

Hilary said, "Colin is a naïve fool."

"I wish you wouldn't say that."

"I'm sorry. He's a fool with a good soul."

As Ted was about to leave the bathroom, Hilary stopped him. "Don't go. Get into the bath with me."

"The bath will overflow."

"Good, good, let it overflow. Let everything overflow."

Thirteen

Ted had to go again to Helsinki for a meeting. The meeting again was not a success. He had a few hours before his plane was to leave for London, and he bought an old map of the city, thinking he would never return.

As he entered the house in London, Hilary met him in the entrance hall. She placed a hand over her chin and said, "Ted."

He said, "Jonathan has died."

"Yes," Hilary said.

He put his case down and looked about the walls of the entrance hall at the collection of old maps. Only after a long while, during which Hilary simply stood before him, did he pick up his case.

Hilary followed him upstairs to their bedroom and, sitting on the edge of the bed, watched him unpack. Distractedly, he handed her the map of Helsinki he'd bought, which she silently unrolled and studied. To break the silence, she said, "Odd how a map of a city one has never been to makes it appear as though it doesn't really exist except in one's mind." She placed the rolled up map on a bedside table.

He asked, "Why is it everything seems to me so meaningful, though, at the same time, I know it has no meaning?"

"What, darling?"

"Our being here in our bedroom, our bed, the—I don't know—heap of your jewelry on the bureau?"

Hilary leaned towards him and kissed his forehead.

"How is Jessica?" he asked.

"She wants to speak with you. Why don't you go and see her? She'd prefer you to go and see her than to ring her, I'm sure."

"Go and see her?"

In his soul, he had known Jonathan would die.

He asked Hilary, "She did say she wants to see me?"

"I'm saying that, because I know she wants to very much."

"Why me?"

"You would find that out."

"I'll get out of this suit," he said, "and shower and dress in clean clothes."

"You make it sound as if you'll prepare yourself."

"Prepare myself to deal with Jonathan's death?"

"I'm sorry," Hilary said. "I'm sorry because I know his death does have a great deal of meaning to you."

She left him, and she thought, let him prepare himself.

Taxis passed but he concentrated on the details. His will always gave way to some other will in him that saw the pigeon feathers against the vast darkness, as if the darkness were a space behind the feathers, as if that vast darkness had a more powerful will than his own. He looked up and hailed a taxi.

This was his longing, to give into the dark, to give into where Jonathan had gone, where everyone would go, where everyone wanted to go. A sense of relief came to him to look into a darkness that promised the incomprehensible, as if the incomprehensible was where the mysteries were kept, as if the greatest longing was for mystery, to give in helplessly to mystery. And that was where Jonathan had gone, that was where he had wanted Jonathan to go.

This thinking made him helpless, a helplessness that came with the memory of himself from the remote past when a nun in a parochial school had made the students at their ink-stained desks believe that we are on earth to die and that in our deaths we enter the eternal, which we must pray to enter, must pray to die and enter.

Looking out at London from the taxi window, he thought that his past religion was so remote from him now it made him wonder that any religion should be so far from life, but it was the religion he was born into and brought up in.

His religion, that religion he was born into and baptized in, that was his religion, and it had been Jonathan's religion too. And that was the religion of the greatest mystery, the very greatest mystery, the mystery of all that made life in the world meaningful.

The world became meaningful through the religion's incomprehensibilities, because of the incomprehensible mystery of the religion's sacraments, its ceremonies of marriages and funerals, its charity, its faithfulness, its pity, its love, and, oh, for the wonder of the Catholic religion, a wonder that made him a Catholic, that he would never, ever deny.

He was, eternally, a Catholic, and that he would never, never give up.

Ted thought, of course he wanted Jonathan not to have died, of course he wanted to see the boy come into the sitting room when he was there with his mother and embrace him, and say, "Ted, Ted."

But Jonathan was dead, was dead, Ted thought with a strange sense of relief, whatever relief that was, which might have been only the relief of being back in London, because returning to London was always a relief to him, but it appeared to him now that London was aware of the death of a boy, and the world of active London appeared to have withdrawn with relief into a world where everyone was at peace.

Yes, Ted was a Catholic, and to be a Catholic was, yes, to be eternally a Catholic, that was what he as a Catholic longed for, but the agony was that there was no eternal life.

Ted closed his eyes, as if London kept shifting as his thoughts kept shifting on his helpless feelings, because he was, Ted Beauchemin was, a person who could not help himself for all that he felt.

He had to give in to his helpless feelings, and his most helpless was the agony, oh, yes, the agony, of longing for what could not be, to believe in what could not be.

He thought, We believe in what cannot be, we love what cannot be.

Out of the taxi to pay the driver, he wanted to say to him, I am a Catholic.

Jessica, her hair pushed back exposing her pale face, opened the door, and, seeing Ted, cried out. For the first time, he noted she had a mole on the side of her neck. She appeared to him someone he didn't know, and the suffering of that someone else meant something to Ted that was unbearable to him, and, his face stark, he felt that all his commiseration was for that someone else he didn't know, in a place where he had never been.

As though, finally, she were with someone who would give her the permission she needed to do what her body impelled her to do, she smiled.

They were standing at the open door. Jessica drew him inside by a hand and closed the door, and, smiling, led him into the library, where Rosemary, the daily, was cleaning.

Jessica asked her, "Will you leave us, Rosemary?"

The daily nodded, but waited.

"Would you like something?" Jessica asked Ted. "Coffee? Tea?"

He shook his head. He hadn't come for coffee or tea. But Jessica asked Rosemary to bring them tea, and she and Ted sat together on the sofa.

Her hands clasped in her lap, Jessica talked as if about a social arrangement. And it seemed to Ted that a fundamental change had occurred in Jessica, and he now saw a woman with the deepest reason for suffering, who had become conventional, even superficial, in her social expression of such suffering.

"Colin left this morning to go to Scotland, where I'll join him tomorrow. There are so few Catholic churches in Scotland, he'll have to ask in Glasgow for a priest. He insists, he insists. I don't know who will be there."

She was not asking Ted to come, and he would not ask to go, and his removal from the services that would encircle the death of Jonathan had, for him, the effect of removing Jessica from them, as if her participation depended on his participation. He could not imagine her as the mother suffering the death of her son, could not even imagine her weeping at her son's funeral and burial.

When she said, "Colin has withdrawn so from everyone," Ted understood that she was excusing Colin for not wanting anyone other than herself and what remained of his family to come to Scotland.

He did not really believe in this Jessica suffering, this anglicized American, whose very title he couldn't take seriously. And also, as refined as she was even now, she didn't look like a woman who could suffer. With every reason to be a suffering woman, he did not see this woman in Jessica, but he did feel deeply that, if not Jessica, there was another, truly suffering woman behind her, another woman digging her fingernails into her cheeks and wailing for all the darkness.

Not for Jessica, but for that other woman, that other woman who was entirely consumed by helpless grief, did Ted—whoever he was—feel commiseration. And when, startling him, Jessica fell towards him and he put out his arms to hold her, he felt it was not Jessica he was supporting, not Jessica whose grief he didn't quite believe in, but that other woman who had so much more reason to suffer, that truly grieving woman, who had a mole on the side of her neck that he had never noticed before. Jessica withdrew only when Rosemary came in with a tray of tea things. Wiping her eyes, Jessica asked her to put the tray on the table before the sofa then told her she could go, and Jessica poured out a cup of tea for Ted, but he left the cup on the tray.

Was it just to be social with the Jessica sitting next to him that he heard himself say to her, "Did Jonathan receive his Holy Communion before he died?"

"Ted, Ted," Jessica cried, leaning towards him, but the cushion under her slanted the other way, and she slipped towards the arm of the sofa with the lap rug over it. Her head pressed awkwardly against the sofa, her hands over her face.

Ted thought he had always, all his life, wanted to express what not he, but another Ted felt, and he had never been able to, never been able to find the words, the gestures. Again, it came to him that all his life he had imagined that where he was was not where he should be, but somewhere else, somewhere different, somewhere really foreign, where he wasn't, and where maybe he wasn't able to go, but where, if he could go, he would find the words and gestures to express what was in him to express, what pressed on him from inside his chest to be expressed—the vast and helpless commiseration of grief.

Combing her short hair back with her fingers, Jessica turned slowly to Ted, mucus running from her nose.

"Can I get you a tissue?" Ted asked.

"In the lavatory just off the hall," she said.

His matter-of-fact going for tissues, pulling them from a box that was encased in a satin, lace-edged cover on a glass shelf in the lavatory and bringing a wad of them back to Jessica, was so incongruous to what he should have been doing to express his commiseration though he didn't know what the expression could be. He almost thought them funny, thought the sofa with the sprung springs funny, thought Jessica asking Rosemary to bring tea funny. And watching her blow her nose, he had no idea, no idea at all, whom he felt such a sense of grief for, because it wasn't for commiseration with Jessica, and, perhaps, it wasn't for the death of Jonathan. He felt a little absurd, but this feeling seemed unreal to him. All his real feelings were elsewhere, he had no idea where.

Jessica stood and looked at the balled up tissues in her hand and then passed Ted to go to the desk behind the sofa, where she threw the tissues into the leather wastepaper basket stamped with gold fleurs-de-lys. "That makes me feel a little better," was all she said.

She was just herself, in her banal house, and he was embarrassed that he suddenly felt nothing for her, and he had nothing to tell her that could help her.

She seemed to become aware that she had to redeem herself from her very house, and she asked, "Ted, do you know what the Latin *ad aeterna non caduca* means?"

The way she asked this, with a quiet tone of submission to the incomprehensibility of it, moved him, and he wished he could help her, but, again, he couldn't. "I'm sorry," he said, "I don't."

"I never did learn any Latin," she said, "and I regret that. Colin knows some Latin. I could ask him, but for some reason I don't want to, because, well, he would know, and I'd rather that no one knew, not you, not I, but leave it unknown. I have to believe that there is something unknowable about it all. I have to. You understand, don't you? I know you understand."

"I?" Ted asked.

She had made herself vulnerable, and he had questioned her vulnerability. She looked down, and he knew he had to go.

He said, "I must go," as though he had important work to do, but really because he was being called away by the world outside. Jessica, not looking up at him, led him through the hall to the front door. She didn't say goodbye, nor did he. He heard the door shut behind him.

That moment with her stayed with him and disoriented him. The disorientation had to do, not with Jessica, but with Hilary, whom he'd been so eager to get back to as if only she would orient him, but who now, he felt, couldn't. Now, no one oriented him, no one but a suffering woman for whom he felt compassion but a suffering woman who did not exist for him in anyone he knew.

Instead of returning to Hilary, he wandered towards Regent's Park. He walked along crowded paths to the rose garden, where he stood among all the other visitors. It was surrounded by a cir-

cle of rough wooden posts from which hung, one
to the other, massive swags, great garlands of roses in full bloom, red, pink, yellow, dropping their
loose petals. Beyond the circle were people extended in all directions, all moving among one
another, to, it appeared, the far, circular horizon
of trees.

Someone called out, "Jonathan."

Fourteen

Ted worked in the pulp and paper sector within the investment bank, which meant managing the firm's relationships with the forest products industry. However much the credit quality of a company was paramount to the bank, even if the company was a little dodgy, the bank was conscientious enough about ethical issues that it refused to underwrite securities in the case of an Indonesian company clear-felling in the Sumatran rainforest. But Ted knew there were companies that were, frankly, criminal and yet issued bonds that were underwritten by banks of a lower reputation than the one he worked for, and the reputation of the bank he worked for was not high. Everyone in the banking world knew of Asian companies trading in thousands of tons of plywood that came from illegal sources in South America using bribery, connections with drug cartels, and death threats. And that plywood ended up in Britain, with many people participating in the transition along the way who were unaware of the original crime. Ted was aware, but how much more unaware was he of other illegalities? It could very well have been that buying socks, shoes, shoe polish—buying, in all innocence, a diamond engagement ring—was to be part of a vast, worldwide network of criminal activity. Who knew what was being invested in from the massive profits gained from drugs, from the sale of stolen arms, from sex slavery, from worse horrors? Soap and talcum powder for babies, diapers?

A meeting in the office of his boss—who had a manager above him, who had a manager above him, each manger on a higher floor of the city office building—centered on whether the debt securities of a company should be underwritten because of the evident corruption of its directors.

Looking at his colleagues' faces, Ted was aware of a wrinkle beside a mouth, a chipped front tooth, hair in an ear.

He said he believed the bank shouldn't underwrite the securities of the company being discussed, and yet he had no doubt that another bank, elsewhere, would.

Ted's usual working day could go on into the night, but today the sky was luminous at a high, thin, vaporous level when he got out of the office building in the city.

Hilary was in the country, in Wiltshire, staying with friends he'd met but didn't really know. The separation would be for only a weekend.

He wouldn't have been able to bear more than a weekend away from her.

But he asked himself if it was because she was away that he thought of Jessica, whom he hadn't seen since that last meeting, as if that meeting had been decisive in the uncertainty of it, if uncertainty could be decisive. Perhaps he thought he couldn't be an open, honest friend of Jessica, if they had ever been open, honest friends, whatever being open and honest meant. There was no reason why he should see her. The reason could not have been anything they shared, because Jonathan was her son, and whatever feelings she had about his death had to be those of a mother, though frankly, he thought she was incapable of grief, but was, after all, a hard woman who abided by the conventions, those that she had learned, and one of the conventions was that she did not express her feelings, not ever in tears, not as an American who intended herself to be British. No, Jessica was not a woman of spontaneity.

It was strange to him that he wanted to see Jessica, because his last seeing her had left him feeling that nothing had been said to move her or him to grieve for the death of Jonathan, if grief was what he would have expected to share with her, and not some other movement that could only be sensed between them. Because there was

something he felt that she must feel, too, and the
something was more than grief. No, she was not
a woman to suddenly allow repressions to rise
up and take her over, and yet, again, she was the
mother of Jonathan, and he had died, and something was in her to be expressed, and he had, yes,
the deep, inexpressible sense of what that was.

The evening was still light when he returned
to Chelsea to drop off his briefcase and change
from his business suit into light tan trousers
and a white shirt and a white cotton jacket. He
felt that he had dressed for the evening out with
friends, but as he thought about which friends
he would like to see for, perhaps, a curry out, he
telephoned Jessica hardly knowing he did, wishing she wouldn't answer. But she did, and she exclaimed, in a way that surprised him for the expression of it, "Ted!"

"I wondered if you might be alone," he said.

"I am," she said. "Colin is in Scotland."

"Then you might like to go out for a curry."

Her voice rose. "Come to me. We'll have a
simple supper. Do come to me."

And a sense of something between them came
over him.

He decided to walk slowly through London,
if not all the way to St. John's Wood, he would
walk until it became late and he'd take a taxi. He

told himself he knew London, but beyond Hyde Park Corner, he lost his way in the streets of Mayfair. There were few people at this hour, and most were getting into cars and driving away. On the facades of the old Mayfair townhouses were shining brass plaques, the offices, seen through half-closed Venetian blinds, deserted for the day. As he walked along South Audley Street, he noticed, within a gap between houses, the open gates to a garden, and, checking that he had more than an hour before he was expected at Jessica's, entered the garden.

It was surrounded by brick mansion blocks with many windows, forming something of a courtyard in brick. And in the courtyard were immense plane trees, the mottled trunks bare to a great height from which hung loosely, long, heavily leafed branches. Paths, with benches along them, led Ted around the garden, past a lawn sprinkler and parterres of red and yellow flowers, and to the back entrance to a church, the neo-Gothic arched window as gray outside as the gray stone of the church. The wooden door was open, and Ted entered.

Only one person was inside: an old priest, his clerical collar too large for his thin neck, sitting in a pew and saying his rosary.

Quietly, Ted walked up the main aisle to-wards the back of the church. And only when he turned round did he recognize the altar rail of marble inlaid with panels of lapis lazuli and, above, the red-and-blue stained-glass window of the Virgin Mother assumed into heaven and radi-ant. And he knew where he was.

Ted sat in a pew. He tried to fix himself on his hands, his fingers, his knuckles, his finger-nails, the cuticles of his nails. He looked up to see the old priest stand and leave the pew and walk toward the altar and stop before the railing. As Ted watched him, the priest turned round to look at him, and Ted felt a moment of alarm that the priest would come to him to ask him why he was in the church. He wouldn't be able to an-swer, and the priest might reproach him for being in a holy place with no real respect for its holi-ness, and ask him to leave. The alarm heightened when the priest walked toward him, his rosary still held by both hands at his waist, the beads and crucifix dangling against his black soutane. And the alarm rose to the level of panic when the priest did stop at the pew just inside of which Ted was sitting and, leaning towards him, say, "If you would like to confess, I'm on duty."

"No, no," Ted said abruptly.

"I'm sorry," the priest said, and was about to draw back.

Ted said, "This is the church where a little boy I was close to was to make his Holy Communion last Sunday."

"Jonathan," the priest said.

"Yes, Jonathan."

"We are all, everyone in the community, grief-stricken, as, no doubt, are you."

Ted could not explain to the priest that he found himself in the church by accident; the priest must have assumed he had come on purpose, for reasons the priest would respect too much to question. Ted saw commiseration in the old man's creased but neatly shaven face. He saw also that the priest was lonely and that he wanted to talk, but Ted didn't know if he should move over to make room for the priest to sit beside him or stand to speak with him, and he felt, now, embarrassed. Sensing Ted's uncertainty, the priest again apologized for intruding on Ted's silence, but Ted said, "Please," and stood to face him at eye level. The priest's lashless eyelids appeared swollen.

He asked Ted, "You came to pray?"

Ted simply looked into the old priest's eyes.

"I spend hours at a time here," the priest said, "praying."

"What do you pray for?" Ted asked.

"I pray that we, every single individual in the world, will be as aware of all the world, united and one, as God is aware in His love for the world."

With a little jerk, Ted said, "Oh."

"I've upset you."

"I'd better go," Ted said, and without looking at him, he pressed past the priest, his shoulder brushing against the priest's chest. He turned back only to nod, his eyes lowered, and he hurried down the aisle and out the door through which he had entered.

Out of the church, Ted sat on a bench in the garden. He rocked back and forth on the bench, then became motionless and sat for a while longer until he got up and walked out of the garden, between the open iron-grill gates, back into South Audley Street, which was empty.

At a distance, he saw Oxford Street, where crowds of people crossed from corner to corner, so many they continued to cross even when the light changed to green and the traffic was held back by their numbers. In Oxford Street, he joined the moving mass of pedestrians, crossing from side street to side street, stalling the jammed red busses and taxis. The late sunlight, now as if descended from on high and sunk to the level of the pedestrians, was shining dully about the hundreds, thousands, of bobbing heads, the heads themselves dark. And he knew that this mass of people came out of the darkness and vanished into the darkness.

A person passing by him stared right into Ted's eyes, and Ted turned his head to follow the person now passing him, and when he looked back ahead of him he saw, coming straight for him so they were about to collide, another person. Stopping short, they stared at one another before they both stepped to the right at the same time, then, frowning as they stared more deeply at one another, they both stepped to the left, pedestrians passing on either side. Swaying a little in their uncertainty of which way to go next, they all at once smiled at one another, and Ted more than ever had that sensation, a pull so strong he felt it as if reaching into his chest to pull his heart out into the open, that he was this person before him. And even when, each orienting himself in different directions, they passed each other, Ted was left with the bewilderment that he was who he was and not someone else shouldering his or her way among the crowd of light-radiating shadows massively moving along the pavement.

Not Ted, not himself, had believed Jonathan would die, but some other Ted.

Fifteen

Waiting for Ted to come to supper, Jessica wandered about the room, telling herself there was something important she must do. Back at the desk, she read the draft of a poem, then put it in a drawer, took it out of the drawer, put it in again, and shut the drawer.

At the door at the back of the hall that opened onto stairs down to the dining room and kitchen, she called, "Rosemary!" but there was no answer. Really, she didn't have anything to say to Rosemary. She walked the length of the hall again to the flight of stairs up to the bedrooms, climbed the stairs, entered hers and Colin's room, and looked about not seeing the bed with its flounces, the bedside lamp with its lace-trimmed shade, the gilded Florentine box on the dressing table, but an interposing blankness. Then she left.

Out on the landing she paused when she saw that the door to Jonathan's room was open. Everything became blank to her except, in that blankness, the open door.

The door, closed by Colin, had been closed since Jonathan's death.

Once again at the door down to the dining room and kitchen, she called for Rosemary who appeared at the bottom of the stairs, a large spoon held in both hands.

"Have you been into Jonathan's room?" Jessica asked.

"Do you want me not to clean there?"

"No, no, do as you have been doing." Jessica remained where she was, and Rosemary began to climb the stairs toward her. "You don't have to come up," Jessica said, yet, as though she had a lot to say, she didn't move, and Rosemary climbed to the top step, just below Jessica, and looked up at her with black, questioning eyes in her smooth Filipino face. "It's just," Jessica said, "that I found the door to Jonathan's room open."

Rosemary said, "I will make sure I close it."

"I don't mean that you should close it." Jessica touched her bottom lip. "I simply wondered why the door to his room was open."

"Don't be frightened of Jonathan's room," Rosemary said. "I put his clothes away, his toys and books, made his bed. Just think that he has gone away for a little while and that he will come back."

"Frightened?" Jessica asked, and stepped away from Rosemary and said, "You can go now, I have a guest coming to supper."

"I prepared some soup."

"Soup will do, thank you."

Rosemary appeared to be uncertain about leaving.

"Thank you," Jessica said.

Rosemary left her just as the telephone rang in her bedroom and she hurried across the landing to it.

Colin asked, "Jessica?"

"Who else could it be?"

"Silly of me."

"Are you coming back to London?"

"Do you mind my remaining a while longer here in Scotland?"

"Stay as long as you feel you must."

"I'm doing whatever I can to have Elshieshields made properly habitable."

"Can we afford that?"

"No, we can't."

She said, "Ted is coming to supper."

"Did you ring him?"

"He rang me."

"I thought he might have been offended that I didn't ask him to Jonathan's funeral and burial and blamed you for that."

"Perhaps he was offended and did blame me."

"Still, he rang you."

"He rang me."

"To see you and ask about Jonathan's funeral and burial?"

"I don't know why, Colin."

"He wants to see you for some reason, and you want to see him for some reason, and I'm glad for that, as I think you have a lot to say to each other."

"I don't know what that could be."

"Well, you are both Americans."

"We're too dissimilar as Americans to have that in common, I think."

"The fact is you were both born and brought up as Americans."

"He's at the door now, knocking."

She rushed down the stairs to the door and opened to Ted, who, large, stood against the evening light.

"Come into the library," Jessica said.

"Colin has stayed in Scotland?" he asked, which was, Jessica knew, his way of asking about Jonathan's funeral and burial there.

"Yes, he's stayed in Scotland," she answered, but she didn't want him to know about the funeral and burial, as if he became someone not intimate enough for him to know, and she added, "and I left him there to return to London, but, here, I'm not quite sure why I came back, as if there is something I must do, if I could only think of what."

"I think I know the feeling."

"What feeling?"

"Of wanting to do something and not knowing what that could be."

"You have that feeling?"

"I think I do."

She said, "Of not knowing what you should be doing?"

"Not knowing," he said.

"Well, there we are," she said.

He said, "Hilary is with friends in the country."

"Where in the country?"

"Wiltshire."

"Lovely, Wiltshire is lovely."

"Yes," he said, "lovely."

"Green hills and sheep on the hills."

He wondered, what am I doing here talking about Wiltshire, which neither of us cares about?

Ted shrugged a shoulder and said, "I feel that I haven't been with Hilary enough lately, what with the amount of work to do. Sometimes I get home only after she has gone to bed, leaving me a cold supper in the kitchen. Or, maybe, that when I am with her, I'm not with her."

"What could possibly come between you?"

Again, Ted shrugged a shoulder.

Abruptly, Jessica walked toward the door to the study as if to leave Ted, but in the middle of the room she stopped and raised her finger to her forehead, thinking, and finally she said, "I haven't asked if you would like a drink."

"No, thanks."

They were standing on a Turkey rug.

She let her hand fall, so her arm hung heavily at her side. "Here I am," she said, "trying once again to keep up some manners, and failing." She sat in the large, stained-leather armchair.

Ted sat at the edge of a deep leather sofa with slanting cushions.

Quietly, he said, "On my way here, I thought I'd walk through London, and I got lost in Mayfair, and found myself, strangely, near the Farm Street church where Jonathan was meant to receive Holy Communion, so I went in. I spoke with a priest there."

"Father Ridge?"

"I didn't get his name. He was kind. He asked me if I would like to confess."

"That is kind."

"Yes, kind, but I suddenly couldn't stay in the church, and I think I must have offended him, I left so suddenly." Ted smiled. "I couldn't bear being there."

"Why?"

It seemed to him he was taking a risk, the risk to give way to feelings they were both aware of, feelings they were both aware of that ran deeper than the death of Jonathan, down where they could easily lose themselves. He did not want to lose himself, not with Jessica, not now, not ever, because that would be to give into all too much— all, all too much.

He said, "I was recently in my dead parents' home, looking through documents, and I came across a photograph of myself at Jonathan's age dressed all in white for Holy Communion, and I couldn't bear the memory. Strange. I threw the photograph away."

Jessica stood and went to a table with bottles of spirits and glasses, and she poured out some Scotch whiskey into two glasses, and approached Ted with one, and handing it to him, she said, "You do want a drink, I know you do, but I'm not going to give you any ice and water in our whiskey," and he, taking the glass, said, "Nor would I dare ask." And he raised his glass to her, and she to him.

She sat again and said, "It is so deep in me, crying out, all that I can't hear." And he felt— what?—a stirring in him that shocked him. So he thought, No, no, and without drinking, as if to hold back from that movement, he placed his glass on the low coffee table between them.

"How is Colin?" Ted asked.

"More upset than I had ever seen him. I'm the one who tries to comfort him, but he won't be comforted. He won't come to London, so I have to go to Scotland to stay with him."

Rosemary came to the door to announce that supper was ready. The table in the kitchen in the basement was simply set. Ted opened the bottle of wine and poured it out and they clicked their glasses, and it was as though they had nothing to say to each other. He silently finished his soup, the spoon scraping against the bowl.

"Do you believe in an afterlife, Ted?"

The somewhat querulous way she asked this seemed to Ted to be British, as if Jessica had assumed the querulousness of an upper class woman who had been brought up to respect the profundities, but not dwell on them. No, Jessica did not dwell.

"I did," he said.

"But you don't now?"

Laughing lightly, he said, "I don't dwell on it. Do you?"

She, too, laughed lightly. "I don't dwell on it."

"What kind of Catholic are you?" he asked.

"I'm not sure I have ever thought about it."

"You don't go to church?"

"No, no, nor does Colin. I wouldn't know what church to go to, nor would Colin, at least in London. I suppose his family used to go to a church in Scotland when he was a boy and church mattered in a family, especially a Scots Catholic. I wouldn't know in what way Colin is Catholic. Does it matter, do you think?"

"Matter?"

"I mean, aren't we all supposed to be Catholic and believe in an afterlife?"

"You were brought up Catholic, so you should know."

"I'm not sure I was brought up to be anything but to be socially advantageous given the world my parents brought me up in."

"What was that?"

"Oh, say, Washington gentry."

"And now you are British gentry."

"Scots, if that means anything."

"What kind of Catholic are you?"

"You know, I would have once asked myself, what kind of Catholic *was* I? Now I ask myself what kind of Catholic *am* I?"

"Because of Jonathan?"

"Yes, because of Jonathan."

"You wanted him to be brought up Catholic."

"Of course we did. Doesn't a Jew want his children to be brought up Jewish?" Why? Why? she thought. "Perhaps his death does make one consider what makes one Catholic."

"Makes me consider, yes, that's for sure."

"What is that you consider?"

"What makes me a Catholic still."

"Tell me what."

"The terrible, terrible, terrible belief in eternity. That's what makes us all Catholics—the belief that we live out our lives here, we live our suffering here, for another life in eternity. A terrible belief because there is no eternity, none, but the belief remains the deepest belief in us, even if we say we don't believe, we do, it's in us. It is our agony."

"Our agony?"

He understood that he had used a word that Jessica never used, and nor did he, he realized, in London, because it was not in Hilary's language. But it rose in him of itself, and it rose in him on an impulse now that he couldn't hold back on, the sudden agony he felt that there was no eternity for this world.

"Agony?" she asked.

And here they were, he thought, two Americans who as Americans were divided by a language in which she would use the word scent and he perfume, she looking glass and he mirror, she distraught and he agony.

"He is dead, Ted, he is dead."

She did not say he passed away, no, she had learned to say he is dead, in a language that had always been hers by social interchange between America and England, because Colin would of course have wanted as his wife someone who already understood that one said he died and not passed away; and the lady she was, he thought, was convincing, thin and elegant, and about her always the sense of dwelling on something, at a slight distance from it.

"Oh, Ted," she said

And then this happened: tears coursed down her face as she stared at him.

She was a woman for whom agony did have meaning, and her pain was to keep a distance from it, to keep a distance from herself.

Sixteen

He did leave Jessica thinking that if anything could help him that was music.

In the Underground from the Saint John's Wood station, he decided he get off at the Baker Street Tube station As though the season had changed, there was now a drizzle in the humid air. He walked to Wigmore Hall, leaving it to chance what was being performed there. A recital by a countertenor was going on, sung not by any-one he had heard of, but Ted liked the high, pure voice of a countertenor. He bought a ticket and had to wait for the intermission before he could enter the hall, so he stood out in Wigmore Street, listening.

To get out of the drizzle, he stepped back in-side as the audience left the hall for the interval and gathered about him on the red carpet. When he saw someone he knew in the crowd, he turned to study the programs and photographs of fu-ture performers on the wainscoting wall, and only on the bell ringing for the second part did he find his way to his seat. There were not many in the audience, so, perhaps, not many had heard the name of the countertenor. Ted's jacket was slightly moist from the outside mist. The singer, dressed all in black, came out and bowed and the audience clapped and the singer sang, and Ted's need for music was greater, he knew as he listened, than the performance.

And, after all, the singer was never able to rise to the total belief that the composer of the song had imagined.

And why did he so like the singing of countertenors? Because there was pity in the voice, in the high, resonant pleading for what no other voice could rise to, a painful pleading of a man alone, for he was alone at the pitch of a voice that wasn't a man's voice, not a woman's voice, hardly a human voice.

He heard *Siede in terra, e piange*.

How was he able to listen to arias from another age, when the singer sang out such lamentations, such high registers of spiritual pain, that Ted felt he was one with the singer, singing such lamentations for tears, such high registers of spiritual pain? But not, no, never in the age he lived in, to be admitted in his own voice, not ever to say, quietly, that there was in him the longing to lament, the longing to register spiritual agony, to sit on the ground and weep.

He could hold himself back from using the word *agony*. And he could because there was nothing in his life that impelled agony in him, nothing but some, oh, sense of fatality, without knowing what that was. Except maybe what he was born with that had no words to express it, and the word *agony* did, and with the word the expression of it in song, because in song, yes, he heard himself weep while kneeling on the ground, in song, agony was the deepest feeling in him.

Agony was among words that needed worlds to make them meaningful, and the worlds had gone, and there was no way of bringing them back, no way of bringing back the Catholic world in which words had meaning, the Catholic world of eternity in our agony, yes, in our agony. But to see in the agony of Jesus Christ nailed to the cross the agony of men. To see in the suffering of Jesus Christ nailed to the cross the suffering men do to one another, the dead in war, the men shackled in the rain, the women raped and lying in their blood, the starving children, the dying in their rags. Our agony of despair for mankind, the agony of Jesus Christ whom we pray to to be our despair, and in his despair pity for the world, that, oh, Jesus, we pray on our knees that our eyes weep your tears.

Seventeen

The evening that Hilary was back from the country they ate in an Indian restaurant they often went to in Marylebone. He had once remarked to Hilary that his mother's cooking had been at best bland, and so he wasn't used to spices. This remark had clearly stayed with her, so every time they were in an Indian restaurant, she asked him if he tolerated hot spices.

"Oh," he said, "the hotter the better."

She smiled a somewhat sad smile, because he was doing his best to amuse.

He said, "I had supper with Jessica while you were in the country."

She asked, "How was it?"

"Strange, I think."

"How strange?"

"I don't know that I can say."

Hilary left this, and as though leaving Jessica to the past she said, "I have the feeling that Jessica won't ever invite us to stay in Scotland, that she'll disappear there."

Ted looked away at a large, round table about which an Indian family were gathered, and for a moment he wondered about Hilary's life in India, and when he looked back at her he thought, Who is she?

Hilary did ask, "Did Jessica say or do anything that you thought strange?"

"Nothing."

"Is that so strange?"

He raised his hands, palms up, as if giving up everything to the sky. "All beyond me."

"What is?"

"Oh, everything."

"I don't understand what that means," Hilary said. "What do you mean by everything? Everything is just a word, because, in fact, you can't have everything. That would mean having every single thing in the world, and that, Ted, is impossible."

He laughed. "Is it?"

She asked, "You're a believer, aren't you?"

"A believer?"

"Only a believer can believe in what can't be, only a believer can believe in everything."

"But I'm not a believer," Ted said.

"Belief is there in you so deep you can't even talk about it."

"No," he said, "it isn't there in me."

"Something must remain in you from having been born and brought up a Catholic."

Ted smiled and added, "And having made my Holy Communion?"

"And everything else that makes a Catholic. You can't have left all that behind."

He said, "What is it to believe? Believe in what?"

Hilary ate and then placed her hand over her mouth, then said, "This is very hot. I don't think you'll want to try it."

Ted thought, You want to say something to someone close to you that you believe is meaningful, as meaningful as any meaning could be in all of life, but this something seems incidental before it is said, so you don't say it. There are very few people you can talk to about what you truly believe meaningful, and Hilary, his wife, was not one of them, and maybe that was best, because what was in him to say was in fact incidental to their sitting together at an Indian meal in a restaurant in Marylebone, in London, England. He knew that Hilary had little sense of what was meaningful, little tolerance of the pretense of what was meaningful to him, and so he held back from saying what he wanted to say to her, or, maybe, to anyone. Because, yes, he was pretentious in his belief in the meaningful, which appeared to him to emanate from the little stainless steel dishes of different curries, of the chutneys, the papadums, the glasses of salty kefir. Everything was meaningful to Ted, but there was no way of communicating that to anyone, especially to Hilary, for whom the food had its own meaning in her Indian past, but not beyond that past enough for her ever to wonder, what does everything mean? She was right in insisting, irritated by him, that everything, all together, didn't exist, or existed only in the possibility of every single thing in the world. He agreed, of course he did, and yet every single thing in the world, every cup and saucer, every knife and fork and spoon, every rug, table and chair and bed, every clock, every pebble, every weed, every tree, every glass of water, every lit match and candle, every pair of scissors, made him aware of everything all together, aware in some way that included every single thing, aware in some way that held together everything all together, aware, maybe, of everything all together beyond the world, somewhere beyond the world that held everything in all the world together.

All of this thinking was due to his visit to Jessica, in some way to his being with her, which had been, yes, strange. Everything appeared to him strange. With Hilary, all he could say about his seeing Jessica was: strange. And perhaps that was all it had been: strange. *Strange* was in some way accountable. Hilary would accept *strange* if there was a lightness to it to make her smile.

Ted asked Hilary about her weekend with friends in the country, and she said, "Rain, umbrellas, gumboots, slickers, and I slipped climbing over a style and fell into a puddle of muddy water."

"That sounds like fun."

"Great fun," she said.

He had Hilary. There was nothing between him and Jessica that he could miss when she moved to Scotland. It would be best if she did move to Scotland, and he didn't see her again. Whatever the feelings he had for her were based on so little. There was, really, no accounting for the feelings, and yet they seemed to be always present to him, shifting around as on some movements in him that didn't quite come together in any feeling he recognized.

Looking at Hilary as she recounted her weekend in Wiltshire, he thought how he had met her after her parents had died and she had had their bodies cremated, as they had wanted. And she had spread their ashes in the garden, so while she gardened she would think of them there, as she remembered them, and that was all.

Gravely, he said, "Jonathan believed."

Almost as a reproach, she said, "He was a boy."

"Yes, a boy, and because he was a boy he believed. He believed in the word *believe*."

"That means something to you."

He appeared to think about this. "Yes, it does."

"Because you still are a believing Catholic."

"No, no." Ted lowered his head and frowned, as if to decide if he was or was not still a Catholic, and he looked up and said, "I'm not, and I have no idea what, really, makes a person a Catholic. I seem to have lost all that years ago when I started travelling, a gap year student wanting to see the world. I saw the world, and that prepared me, I suppose, for work in the investment bank. No, I wouldn't be able to say in what way I remain a Catholic, if I remain one at all. But, yes, that Jonathan did believe means something to me, and there must be a reason for that."

"Why did you ask him to pray for you?"

"Did I do that?"

"I heard you."

"When?"

"At the last garden party Jessica and Colin gave. Jonathan was ill and you went up to him to see him, and when I came up to fetch you to go home, I heard you, from the landing, ask him to pray for you."

"Did I?"

"I heard you." She smiled and said lightly, "I hit my shoulder against the doorjamb as I turned away, as I thought whatever was happening between you two should remain with you. Still, I did hear you."

"Yes, when he was in bed and sick, I thought it would help him if I asked him to pray for me."

"Then he would have thought you believed."

"He would have, yes." He nodded. "Yes, he would have."

Hilary raised her chin and said, "An innocent and pure boy would have had his prayers answered in full." She laughed, hardly opening her lips. "You can be sure, Ted, that the prayers of a dying boy have been heard and answered. You can be sure that you've been saved."

"Saved?"

"That eternity is yours."

Eighteen

Colin met Jessica with the car at the train station at Dumfries. In the distance, under the
bright blue sky, were smooth, stark, purple-brown
mountains.

The wires of a pylon stretched to another pylon in the distance, and from that to another in
the farther distance, and from that to a pylon on
the side of a bare, purple-brown mountain, and
no doubt wires stretched from that pylon to another that was out of sight.

Colin appeared so very alone. He didn't even
glance at her when she got in beside him, but neither did he start the engine.

"Of course," he said, "you have every right to
blame me."

"I don't blame you, and I will not have you
blaming yourself."

"It's only you who can stop me from doing
so."

She knew what effort this required of Colin,
an effort he had had in her absence worked himself up to, as though he had had to be on his own
to be able to. In all his vagueness, she had never
heard him admit he was wrong, never heard him
admit he had failed in anything, because such an

admission would give too much importance to himself.

"Then I'll do what I can do," she said.

"Thank you."

Driving, Colin matter-of-factly informed Jessica of the problems he was attending to at Elshieshields, with dry rot and wet rot and a leaking roof. He also told her that yet again a fox had got into the chickens, so he would stop having chickens. Feeding the hens and collecting the eggs had been one of Jonathan's pleasures, and Colin was aware of this, but Colin was not, as she was, a sentimental person, and she relied on his being unsentimental. It occurred to her that she had also always relied on his never being wrong, of his never having failed in anything.

The drive into the park of Elshieshields was made dark and narrow by overgrown rhododendron.

"It will be difficult to keep Elshieshields going," Colin said. "I shall do it, even if that means selling London."

"Then I think you'll have to sell London," Jessica said.

"Would you mind living here?"

"I would do whatever you decide to do."

"Thank you again," Colin said.

Jessica needed Colin, she needed him for his, yes, cultural superiority. As a minor expression of her belief in his superiority, she said, "I don't know Latin, but you do."

"I wouldn't consider myself a civilized person if I didn't know some."

"What does *ad aeterna non caduca* mean?"

"You should know, if not from Latin, the English, caducity."

"I don't. What does it mean?"

"Transitory."

"And the Latin?"

"I would say something like: the eternal, not the transient."

Elshieshields was a stone castle, in part a stark tower, and, yes, there were ravens in the Scottish pines. In the sitting room, Jessica looked at the ravens flying into and out of and into the pines. She was alone.

She had to find it in herself, she thought, a way to start a life here, or anywhere, with Colin, or without Colin if he disappeared, as he always seemed about to do. She didn't know where he was, and perhaps that didn't matter. It didn't matter to her that she was alone because she had always been alone, in a way deeper than any social life she had tried to live. She could do that, she could be sociable, more than Colin, who was not at all sociable. But, strange, she didn't think of Colin ever suffering his being alone, as though that had always been a condition of his life, and he quietly lived all the conditions of his life. And she must do that, but live the conditions of her life in Scotland.

And this occurred to her, that Colin was not a vague person, and neither was she, or she tried not to be.

To her, England was a country of particulars. And as much as she tried to concentrate on the particulars of the very day, that her husband liked kippers for breakfast, they always appeared to float on some vast generalization, on the generalization that was the weakness of her poetry. The vast sublime, the American sublime, on which, she thought, America was founded and would never, ever realize—never, but that she tried to bring down to, what? the kippers her husband liked for breakfast, here, with him in Scotland, where she heard rain had begun to fall against the panes.

If she were to continue writing poetry, she would make the smell of the upholstery of the seat in a train compartment in the heat of summer the grounding of her poem.

Rain fell on the multi-paned windows of the sitting room, and she went to one window to look out. Attached to the frame on the outside was an old barometer, which indicated: RAIN.

She smiled to herself.

Somewhere in her, she thought, was a hard woman, perhaps even a businesswoman, as there had been something of a business sense, but not altogether hard, in her marrying Colin. The marriage had ended with the death of Jonathan and his burial in the family tomb, so they would now have separate bedrooms, and, too, separate friends—if Colin had any friends, or rather if she did. With the end of their marriage and her life as lived with Colin, she would find that business sense and do something that would make sense of her life in rainy Scotland, even if it were to open a boutique in the abandoned stables and sell tartans, with the history of each tartan attached.

She wondered if she would need permission to sell the royal tartan.

Walking quickly around the room, as if about to leave but unable to leave, Jessica pressed her hands to her breasts, her face, her hair, again and again.

She sensed Colin come into the drawing room, and she turned to him, her back against the wall.

"Are you not well, darling?" he asked.

"Oh," she said.

"Shall I fetch you a tissue?"

"Thank you, darling. In the lavatory on the landing."

Colin came back with the tissues, and she wiped her cheeks and blew her nose.

He said, "You need to rest."

"I don't know what I need."

"I wish I could give you that."

"You do, as much as I could expect from anyone, and that is very much, very much."

He came close to her and leaned the side of his head against hers and said, "Thank you," and Jessica kissed his forehead.

She said, "I should have stayed in London. There is so much to do there. Will you drive me to the station tomorrow?"

They had pre-prandial drinks in the drawing room, in the dining room supper prepared by the wife of the couple who lived off the kitchen, and coffee in the library, with a bright fire in the fireplace. Rain fell throughout, and all night, Jessica, in bed, trying to write a poem in her head, using the words *great, grand, sublime*, which, she thought, were such overwhelmingly meaningful words, but which were false because they did not correspond with anything in the world, nor beyond the world in galaxies of stone and gas and celestial dust. So how did she dare to use such

words, to think them, to feel them, because they
were utterly false?

And yet, she thought, she did want to see Ted
Beauchemin.

Colin willingly drove her to the station for
the train back to London, where, too, rain was
falling, and as she waited in a queue for a taxi,
she saw the lights in the dark shine on the black
taxis as if with a need for a London she had once
hoped to make her home, but which she had
failed to do.

Nineteen

On his return home from Saturday morning at work, where a report was circulated about drastic cuts in earnings forecasts across the pulp and paper sector, Hilary told Ted that Jessica, back from Scotland, had rung. Jessica wanted to speak to him.

"About what?"

"She didn't tell me. She's in London for a while before returning to Scotland."

Ted hesitated, not wanting Hilary to assume he was eager to speak to Jessica.

He said, "I'll ring her later."

"She seemed eager to speak to you."

"Later," he insisted.

Hilary, as she often did, touched Ted's cheek.

He clasped the hand Hilary held to his face, put his other hand about Hilary's waist, and he said, trying to be light-spirited, "Let's you and I go out and have lunch, just the two of us."

"Won't you ring Jessica?"

"I will, after lunch with you."

But, entering the restaurant off St. Martin's Lane, Ted thought he would get Hilary seated then excuse himself and say he had to go to the men's room, and, instead, would ring Jessica from his mobile telephone. He didn't, telling himself to put Jessica out of his mind and think only of being with Hilary.

He was almost able to put Jessica out of his mind, here in the small room with old, dark wainscoting, at a table covered with a heavy, stiff, white cloth, watching Hilary eat oysters from a bed of crushed ice and samphire and pause now and then to sip light, bright wine from a large but delicate goblet with a long, thin stem. She took up a dripping oyster and with a little fork disengaged the body from its shell, squeezed lemon juice onto it from half a lemon wrapped tightly in muslin, and stuck out her tongue as she brought the oyster to her mouth and tipped the pale, loose body over her bottom lip, then swished it about her mouth and swallowed. She dropped the empty shell and smiled at Ted. "I'm eating them all up," she said.

"They're all for you," he said, but a second later, her incidental remark, which was meant to express her pleasure, and his remark, which was meant to express his delight in her pleasure, made him consider: she did not see that she took for granted her place in a privileged world. Wasn't it in Hilary's very being that it never occurred to her that banks did anything in the world but good, because they allowed such lunches? And wasn't it all just this in Hilary that had made her so reassuring to Ted and that made her, now, so solidly happy, a little like a Victorian English lady, he thought, unassumingly benefiting from the riches of the empire?

He stared at Hilary eating oysters at this table scattered with empty shells here and there where they'd been dropped among the plates, some turned over to the gray scrotal roughness of their exteriors, some lying with their smooth white labial interiors exposed, and he wondered how she could not know more about the world in which they led their daily lives, in which she was able to take such pleasure.

But how could he be thinking this about Hilary, who was in fact more generous in her attention to others than he was, he who would never volunteer in a hospice garden, who had no pathetic friends whom he asked over, who was, as she was not, demanding in his selfishness? It was wrong, it was everything he didn't want, to see her as no more than someone created by her world now in this restaurant because she was no more than what her world had created of her.

Wiping her fingers on a large, starched, white napkin, Hilary sat back to let the waiter clear the table for the next course.

Put everything out of your mind about Hilary, Ted told himself, but her pleasure.

She asked, "I wonder where, at this time of the year, the oysters come from?"

"Don't ask."

Don't ask where the oysters came from. Don't ask where the wine came from, where the glass for the bottle came from, where the paper for the label, where the ink for the printing. Don't ask where the clay for the china plates came from, where the linen for the tablecloth and the napkins, the salt, the pepper. And don't ask about the people who served them—the waiter, the busboy, the people behind the doors to the kitchen who scraped the leftover food from the dishes, the garbage man who carted off the swill, the workers at the stinking dump. And beyond these people, don't think about the people, hundreds of them and all invisible to him, who made it possible for him and Hilary to sit here at this table and eat and drink wine. Don't ask about them, though they were rising up all around him as if to undo the Victorian lady of her ignorant and luxurious indulgences.

When she asked, "What's the matter?" Ted laughed, or tried to.

She pulled the cold, wet, green bottle of wine from the silvery wine cooler standing by the table and, reaching across the table, filled Ted's glass.

The waiter served the second course, grilled wild Scottish halibut, and this, tasting of the depth of the sea, was all Ted should have needed to be reassured of life at a restaurant table with Hilary. He wasn't hungry, but he ate so that she wouldn't again ask him what the matter was. And he told himself he was pleased that Hilary prolonged the meal by ordering a brandy with her coffee.

But looking at him closely for a moment before she sipped her brandy, Hilary put the glass on the table and said to him, "We'll go home."

"No. I'll have a brandy too."

"You're making me act falsely, Ted. I'm trying to act in the way I know you want me to act."

"I really do want to join you in a brandy," Ted said, and he raised a hand to a waiter. When the glass was placed before him, he didn't lift it, he studied it, and was drawn into concentrating in greater and greater detail on it, on the fine circles of light that ran round the thin rim.

"Ted."

There was in Ted, and not so deeply that he didn't recognize it in the world of his work, the knowledge of corruption in all that mattered

when dealing with money. And there was a deeper sense of corruption which occurred to him in a
moment of self-awareness, a sense he would have
been too embarrassed to admit to anyone, even
to Hilary. But that was sinful—sins that anyone
might have told him were no longer sins, at most
heightened adventures in sex, but were to him
sins of sexual unfaithfulness to the person one
loved with someone else whom one didn't love,
sins against Hilary. Not, oh not, that he would
judge anyone for sinning, judgment was not in
him, not in Ted Beauchemin. He would never
have asked Hilary if, in her past, she had had af-
fairs. He didn't want to know, and he was sure
that she was in their marriage as faithful in her
love and sex as he was, as faithful, he thought,
as he was sure his mother and father had been,
all their lives together. No, he did not judge, and
never thought that anyone he met was guilty of
sin, no. Not anyone, no, but everyone all together
was guilty, all the world was guilty.

And that world guilt wasn't because there
was such unfaithfulness in love and sex in the
world, suggestions of which came to him when,
in a café on a trip to foreign countries, he over-
heard, but pretended not to hear, even among
colleagues. Nor was there that worldwide guilt
because of sexual squalor, of destructive drugs,

of rape, of murder, of slavery. Nor the destitute and starving salvaging in massive landfills, nor the devastations of forests left to stumps, nor the open mining in vast pits and leveled mountains, nor the detritus of garbage rising on the sea tides, nor the oil wells in deserts of black sand, nor polluted drinking water, not lakes filled with dead fish, nor the pelican covered in oil slick, nor the massacre of bees, nor the warmer and warmer air cracking up icebergs. No, no, it wasn't the promiscuity of guns, of automatic rifles, of bombs, of weapons of mass destruction, of poisoning and burning gases that were the sins that made the world guilty. No, nor torture, nor bodies buried in pits they had been forced to dig, nor beheadings, nor a soldier burned alive in a locked cage, nor a woman stoned to death in a football stadium for everyone to watch. No, nor was the guilt of the world caused by the helpless poor, by the evictions of families from their homes out on the street with their furniture, by the homeless beggars. Nor was war the world's greatest sin. No. All these the world bore, year after year, and would bear. No. The deepest and grandest sin was too deep, too grand to call up in name even as the source of all the world's guilt, but whose condemnation was that the hopeless world wanted to die.

He lifted his eyes to her, and saw, in detail, the tiny globules of mascara on her lashes, the faint smears of makeup on her nose and cheeks. He had seen her cosmetics on her bureau, had seen her make up her face, but even so he had always had the impression until now that her face was as natural as she was.

"All I need," he said, "is to go to the gents' and splash cold water on my face."

Smiled at politely by waiters on his way, he went, lurching a little, down to the lavatory, where he did splash cold water on his face, then dried himself with a small towel taken from a pile left on a shelf above the washbasin and patted his hair into place.

He thought, the thought more of a feeling: This is what we want, we want the entire world to die, not because in the death of this world there is a promise of another world, better than this world. There is no other world.

He took from the inside pocket of his jacket his mobile telephone. There were two messages on it that he was sure had to do with work, but he would give no attention to them now. As though it was not his, his hand pressed the buttons to ring Jessica, and he noted on that hand the wrinkles of his knuckles, the cuticles of the nails, the veins.

When he was back at the table, Hilary told him she had asked for the bill, which she had paid.

Ted asked, "Do you mind if I let you go off and I go on to see Jessica?"

He saw this came to her as a surprise, but she said, as he knew she would say, "But didn't I urge you to ring her?"

Twenty

In the tearoom at Fortnum & Mason, Ted saw Jessica before she saw him, sitting against a wide wall painting of eighteenth-century English tea merchants in China. Her elbows on the edge of the table, her forearms raised, she turned the gold bracelet that had fallen almost to the elbow of her slender arm or flicked the short, fair hair away from her ears and played with her tiny gold earrings. When she saw Ted, she half stood.

"If you haven't yet ordered, do you mind not having tea?" he said. "I'd like to walk. We can walk around Green Park."

Her slender body—neck, shoulders, back, small of back, narrow buttocks—made an undulant motion as she rose.

Under the large, dense, dark-green trees of the park, Jessica said, "Let's sit here," and they sat together under a tree.

A group of boys passed by them, and at a distance behind the boys another boy was running toward them, calling, "Ted, Ted," and the boy in the group who was Ted stopped and turned to wait for the boy running toward him. They grasped each other's arms and, excited, the boy who'd called out Ted said something so important that both of them ran off quickly, away from the other boys.

Jessica tried to smile with the fine corners of her lips. And he smiled, too.

He said, "You wanted to see me."

Jessica delicately touched her nose as if to give poise to her saying, "Well, I felt that you might want to see me."

"Oh, I do."

And yet, they were silent.

But he did not want a serious talk with Jessica, any attempt at such talk false, and he realized he often did feel false when he talked to her about a subject of some seriousness, such as politics, which she knew well, but which he knew only in terms of his work at the investment bank.

And, as though she, too, was aware of not wanting to enter into talk that would be too serious, or, perhaps, too personal, but that, really, would be too embarrassing to enter into, because he felt that they were, together, always on the edge of being false with each other, she said, as a way of deflecting from themselves, "You're very lucky to have Hilary," but this reflected back on themselves, sitting stiffly on the bench.

"I don't know how I would live without her."

Looking away from him, she said, "Go, go back to her now. I don't want to make a fool of myself and use words that have no meaning to us, to anyone."

"I understand," he said, and he looked at his watch and said, "In fact, I should get to the office."

"You worry about your job there, don't you?"

"Yes."

"I suppose anyone working in an investment bank would."

She seemed to know a lot about the financial situation of the world. She had that kind of mind.

He stood, and they said goodbye, but with the sense that whatever reason there had been for their meeting was left open, because they didn't shake hands. So, when he turned and walked a little away, he was not surprised to hear her call him, "Ted," and he turned back, and as if he had gone a long distance from her, she called out, "I can't any longer." And he saw himself as if from the distance go back to her and sit again on the bench, and he saw himself hold her in his arms, saw her press her forehead to the side of his head.

She drew back and shook her head so her short, fine hair shook. She bit her lower lip, which she slowly released from her teeth, then she said, thoughtfully, "We so long for what can't be. Tell me, what is it? You know."

He laughed a laugh that was no more than opening his mouth and breathing out *ha*, and he said, "Our Holy Communion?"

This made her laugh, too, lightly.

"When do you go back to Scotland?" he asked.

"As soon as I can get some pressing things done in London."

He had to bring them down from where they were, high up together where people shouldn't go, so he said, "Tell me about Elshieshields."

He thought he had never felt as false as he was now with Jessica, and she, he was sure, felt the same.

"Well, it's a castle, and, you know, it has a ghost."

"A ghost?" he asked, and he knew she was no more interested in telling about the ghost than he was in hearing about it.

"She appears at night and sets the clock in the sitting room ringing, no matter what the time is. Colin grew up with her setting the clock to ring, he's reassured by this, and so, I suppose, am I. So when the clock starts to ring, we wake up and, however far we are in the bedroom, we listen, and when the ringing stops, we go back to sleep. Colin makes sure the clock is always wound so it will ring. Colin can be light-spirited, you know, and I become light-spirited with him."

"I'm glad."

"I hope that our little girl ghost will go on ringing the clock when we move to Scotland from London."

"You'll have lots to do."

"Lots."

He knew she did not mean that she had lots to do when she raised a hand and made a gesture as if dismissing the very reason for her having wanted to see him, and said, "Well, it can't be."

He agreed with her. "It can't."

Her tone was hard when she said, "As I'll be leaving London for good, perhaps it'd be best if we were to say goodbye now."

"I'm sorry," he said with a softness to his voice, "but I suppose so."

He watched Jessica walk away.

He continued to sit on the park bench as if stillness were the only possible outward expression of his feelings, wondering why there should be such helpless longing in the sight of sunlight and shadows through the trees.

But he saw Jessica walking towards him.

He stood and a little shock went through him when she said, "Ted," in a voice of calling him to attention.

"Yes," he said, attentive.

"I want you to come to the Farm Street Church with me. That's why I wanted to see you."

"Now?"

"Now. I want us to go together and ask Father Ridge to give us Communion."

"Jessica, I—" he began.

But she insisted, "Do this for me. Do it for us. We want it."

"I'm not sure what we want," he said.

But she was walking ahead of him, for him to follow.

And there was nothing to say in the taxi.

What would they do together in the church?

Imagine them kneeling side by side, and a priest holding out the consecrated hosts to them.

Did death mean anything? A foolish question because he of course knew the answer.

To long for what couldn't be.

That was a great longing.

The main doors of the church in Farm Street were locked. He followed Jessica to South Audely Street to enter the brick courtyard and along the path to the back door of the church, but that, too, was locked. Ted followed Jessica to the rectory and stood behind her when she rang the bell, and they waited, and the door was opened by a young Black man wearing a cassock and the collar of a Jesuit.

"Is Father Ridge in?" Jessica asked.

"Is it urgent?"

"It's urgent. Tell him I'm Jonathan's mother."

"The boy who died," the young priest said.

"The boy who was to receive his Holy Communion," Jessica said, "but he died before."

"I truly am sorry," the young priest said. "I'm sure that Father Ridge would want to speak with you, but, you see, Father Ridge is in Rome. Is there anything I can do for you?"

Jessica said, "We want to receive Holy Communion."

His hand on her shoulder, as if to draw her back, Ted said, "Please, Jessica."

"Now?" the priest asked.

"Yes, now," Jessica insisted.

"I don't see how I could do that."

"Do you mean, have I been to confession, have I purified myself to receive the Holy Sacrament? No. I'm impure. I'm a sinner."

The priest said, quietly, "I am so very sorry," as he began to close the door.

As if over Jessica's head, Ted said, "Jonathan wants us to receive for him."

Closing the door more, so he was only half visible in his black cassock, the white of his collar showing about his neck, the priest said, "I am so sorry," and he closed the door fully.

And there they were, Ted and Jessica, holy fools, Ted thought—holy fools and, no doubt from the young priest's vision of them, just fools. The priest had been right to close the door on them.

They sat on a bench in the courtyard, under a large plane tree. Ted would leave to Jessica what they would do next, if there was anything to do next. Jessica was slouched on the bench, a silk scarf loose about her, her eyes staring.

Ted noted, on the ground, an envelope with a stamp, and on it a name and an address, but too damp to be deciphered. He picked it up and saw that the envelope had been opened and that a letter was still inside. He let it fall to the ground then he reached down for the envelope at the point of his shoe, and he opened the envelope to remove the letter and unfold the one sheet. He read out:

Dear Funny Face,

When will I see you next? I can't wait, I really can't. Waiting strains my pants, so I think they'll fly out, like on a spring, and what will I do if you're not here? Do you long for me? I hope you

do because if you don't, I'll have to find another
Funny Face. But you're the only one I want. No
other Funny Face will know how much I long for
you to hold you and kiss you and, oh, so much, so
much, that I feel that I will die in you, just die,
and never, ever come back.

Your ever longing Ugly Face

A prickling sensation rose up in Ted as if from all his body and tightened his scalp, and he held out his hands to protect himself from a presence that, oh, beamed out at him, a light too bright for him to see.

An elderly, pale man in baggy trousers and an open-collared shirt and jumper came to them and said, "Please excuse me," and Ted recognized the priest whom he had spoken to in the church some weeks before. The priest said, "I couldn't leave you as you were left. I understand what you must feel about wanting to fulfill what Jonathan couldn't. I'm afraid I can't offer you Holy Communion, the communion hosts haven't been consecrated, but would you like to go into the church?"

Jessica answered for Ted, or so he felt she did when she said, "Thank you. For a moment."

Again, Ted followed Jessica and the priest to the back entrance, where the priest unlocked the door and stood aside for Jessica and Ted to enter, and there, in the stony silence, the stained-glass window over the high altar shone in blue light, for the window was dedicated to the Holy Virgin Mother.

The priest said, "Would you like me to bless you both?"

Ted said, "Thank you, Father."

Jessica placed a hand on her bosom and Ted lowered his head while the priest blessed them, and the priest showed them out of the church and closed the door after them.

If Ted were ever to think of her, long after a separation that he sensed they both understood was forever because nothing now held them together, he would remember this moment, it seemed to him, of immense space, and they were in that immense space.

She said to him, "Well, goodbye." She turned away but when he called, "Jessica," she raised an arm, then dropped her arm and, with her fingers making a small gesture, she walked on.

And that other Ted appeared before him, the Ted who watched him closely.

Twenty-one

He walked back through St. James's Park, where he stopped for a moment to study the strange ducks on the pond, then he walked out of the park and through Belgravia to where Chelsea began.

He found Hilary in the sitting room, in the middle of the sofa, a round, shallow basket in her lap from which she chose from a heap different-colored glass beads to thread on a cord. He sat across from her in an armchair.

She said, "I've had these Tibetan ceramic beads for years. I bought them in India, and only now thought of making a necklace out of some of them as a gift to a little girl."

"What little girl?"

"You wouldn't know her. She comes to speak to me in the garden of the hospice."

"You've had the beads from since you were in India?"

"I have, yes."

"I hope they bring back happy memories."

"Oh yes."

She wouldn't ask him about Jessica because she allowed him that relationship, but he imagined she must nevertheless wonder why Jessica had wanted to see him. Hilary picked up a bead, held it up to examine the fine blue stripes in the white ceramic, then slipped it onto the cord; it clicked faintly against the other beads.

Looking at her, he felt sorry for her for being married to him, for loving him, as he knew she did.

"You look tired," Hilary said. "You should go upstairs and rest."

Ted stood. "I've got work to do."

She said, lightly, "Then you must do it."

"Of course I must do it, and I have you to thank for insisting. What would I do without your insisting?"

Hilary threw the unfinished necklace onto the heap of beads in the basket on her lap and laughed an almost raucous laugh. "My God," she said, "you make me imagine that you're about to die and I'm keeping you alive."

"You are," he said.

"Please don't."

"Don't what?"

"Embarrass me."

"Who else could hear?"

"It's enough for me to hear," Hilary said.

"But you do."

"Please, Ted."

He was at the doorway into the hall, about to leave, but he said, as if the thought had come to him suddenly, "What will save us?"

"This is very deep, Ted. You're tired and I'm tired. You know I'm not used to such talk, which, yes, is embarrassing to me, and should be to you."

"I think I'm somewhere beyond being embarrassed."

"I think you always have been."

"Is that bad of me?"

"I'd even say it's good for you, good, perhaps, for Americans, who are so far beyond embarrassment that they think they can make the most embarrassing statements and believe that somewhere far out there they're sincere."

"If you're saying that Americans don't have a sense of irony, I pass, because I've never been good at irony."

"And I wouldn't want you to be. Not you. You can embarrass me, I don't mind, but I couldn't bear you feeling embarrassed by what you feel is in fact sincere. You are sincere. I couldn't bear your being ironical. Thank God you're not British."

Ted ran a finger up and down the doorjamb, and he smiled. "Thanks," he said.

"Go up to your work."

"Not yet. If you're going to allow me to embarrass you, I will."

"Ted, Ted, sometimes I do think you are a silly boy I love."

"Then, silly boy that I am, tell me why you love me."

"I'm not up to your question."

"Try."

Hilary said, "Well, it's very simple why."

"Oh?"

He was testing her, and because she knew that she would always rise above his tests, she enjoyed this.

She said, "Look at you."

"Look at me?" he asked.

She said, "Go to your desk."

But Ted now leaned against the doorjamb. "What do you see, looking at me?"

"Do I have to tell you?"

"I suppose it would help me to know."

"There you are," Hilary said, "and what do you think it means to me that here I am threading beads onto a cord but, I can tell you this, every single bead is wonderful."

"Wonderful?" Ted asked.

"Wonderful."

"Am I wonderful to you?"

"You are."

He thought she would laugh, but she didn't, and neither did he, though he waited a moment, as if intending to say something more, then he said, "I have to go to Helsinki again tomorrow."

Hilary said, "I thought your last meeting there went so badly, you'd never go back."

"Did I tell you that?'

"You did."

"I didn't think I'd go back," Ted said, "but now I'll go try to put right what went wrong."

Hilary pursed her lips, which she always did when considering something she imagined important, and Ted wanted her to say all that she considered important, but she said nothing.

Ted said, "Tell me about the girl you're making the necklace for."

Hilary said, "She helps me in the hospice garden. I'm trying to help her recover from a horror."

"What horror?"

"She was raped. The rapist threatened to cut off her breasts if she didn't give in to him. She talks to me about it all, talks and talks."

"And what do you say?"

"I ask her to help me dig up the irises."

"You're helping her."

"Go to your work," Hilary said.

But he returned to her and almost spilled the basket of beads by coming to her and reaching down to put his arms about her shoulders and press his forehead against hers.

"Now that I've made myself a silly girl, go," she said.

In his study, Ted sat for a long while at his desk. It was wrong, he knew, but he couldn't make himself read the pulp, paper, and packaging review that had just come in. He couldn't read it because he felt he would be alerted to possible investments that he could not recommend. Never before had he felt quite so exposed to the world by his work, as if the world were aware of him now, and he was in a position to do more damage to the world that the world had so far withstood, or had tried to withstand.

Oh, tried and failed.

There they were, he thought, the bronze and stone monuments to war: at Hyde Park Corner, the monument to the Royal Artillery and the soldier leaning against it, his arms outstretched under his cape, wearing a helmet and puttees, and his machine gun at his side, commemorating forty-nine thousand and seventy dead artillery in the Great War, a monument that Ted always turned to with a shock when passing it on a bus. And the monument to the Royal Marines, in a pith helmet and his rifle and bayonet on the ready, standing near Admiralty Arch. And the two statues of standing soldiers with high casques, one with a rifle and the other with a sword, in Hobart Place. And the war memorial to the London troops near the Royal Exchange and the five soldiers from the Royal Tank Regiment standing in bronze in Whitehall. And the Imperial Camel Corps on the Embankment and the monument to the Foot Guards in Saint James's Park, and the lone Gurkha, holding his rifle and bayonet at attention in the Horse Guards Avenue, and, oh—

Ted read the review through the tears that filmed his eyes, because the only way to read it was through tears.

Concern over economic conditions especially has led us to review exposure of the sector to North America.

That he, Ted Beauchemin, understood this all at once surprised him. That he should understand such terms as debt capital markets, for which he was responsible in his team, seemed to him so strange that he wasn't sure he did understand it—or what he did persuading corporates to issue bonds to be underwritten by the bank he worked for. He did understand. But there was a meaning to his work that he didn't understand, a meaning that was beyond him, not just because the higher levels of capitalism were too high for him, but because the meaning rose much higher, beyond anyone's understanding—rose so high he felt from the height of that ultimate but incomprehensible meaning that investment-grade bonds or non-investment-grade bonds or high-yield or junk bonds were meaningless; felt, from the height of that vast, ever-expanding, ultimate and ultimately incomprehensible meaning that all his work, all work in all banks, was of this world only and of great damage to the world. From that height, he read:

Grades most exposed are those with high transatlantic trade such as newsprint, pulp, coated fine paper, and linerboard. Least exposed include cartonboard.

Risen above himself so there were two Teds reading, the language of the review became abstract to the Ted above. The particulars of newsprint, pulp, coated fine paper and linerboard seemed to occur like disconnected objects in that abstract space. And as the Ted below turned the pages of the review, putting those objects into the context of the U.S. and world economy, the Ted above saw five hundred seventy thousand tons of carbonless copy paper, fifty thousand tons of thermal paper, one hundred forty-four thousand tons of coated fine paper float free. The Ted above read along with the Ted below that a company in the U.S. had a printing division profitable in producing color paint cards, though this was not considered core in the long run. Around the Ted above color paint cards began to fly about in the air, red, blue, orange, green, yellow. Corrugated board, folding cartons, newsprint rose up from the review, and filled the air along with the color paint cards.

While the Ted below studied such statements as *globalization likely to reduce price differentials between markets*, the Ted above found himself surrounded by sheets of coated magazine papers peeling off from the gardening magazines Hilary read.

When the Ted above saw the Ted below stop to study a paragraph which read *the yields on the Finnish stocks in particular look attractive*, he understood why the Ted below should have to go to Helsinki.

Twenty-two

At the memorial service in St.-Martin-in-the-Fields for an old friend of her parents, Hilary was attentive to the people in pews before her in order to keep her thinking fixed on them. She studied the different hairdos of the women, and, as though this had to do with her attentiveness and not with thinking, she asked herself when hats ceased to be worn on occasions such as memorial services.

She recalled her mother telling her that, invited to a garden party at Buckingham Palace, she hadn't worn a hat and was never invited again. Hilary had no interest in royal garden parties, but she did wonder if women no longer wore hats even there.

She also recalled her mother saying to her, one does not say *perfume*, nor *mirror*, and, God help us, not *serviette*, and her asking, why? And her mother answering, they are French words.

Hilary had received an announcement for the service simply because she was her parents' daughter and should be invited. And she was attending perhaps for no other reason than that she was her parents' daughter and through them had a distant sense of obligation to go.

She stood to join the congregation in the singing of a hymn.

At the end of the service, the descendants of Lady Charlotte, from an old, disheveled son in a dark suit to plump twin girls chatting to each other, processed down the central aisle and out of the church, and the people in the pews, congesting, followed. Among them, Hilary saw the bald head of Colin Kerr.

Out on the porch of the church, she shook hands with each of the relatives standing in something of a row, then she turned to where Colin was standing by a pillar and looking out at the gray day extended over Trafalgar Square. She wasn't sure he wished to see her, or, really, if she wished to see him. She had not written to him about Jonathan because she found it impossible to get herself to write. Standing next to the pillar and looking out, Colin appeared so very alone, though he knew everyone at the memorial service in much more intimate ways than Hilary. Perhaps he chose to be alone. She thought she should simply pass him by and descend the stone steps down from the porch. This would relieve her of the embarrassment of not having written, and if he happened to see her pass, he would be relieved of having to pretend a relationship they didn't really have. Glancing at him sideways as she was passing, she thought he did look very different, and at that moment he too glanced sideways and their eyes met.

Hilary stopped, one foot before the other, but she said nothing, and she didn't approach him. She saw—no, not the sadness she expected in his stark face, his cheek bones prominent in his white cheeks, dark circles about his large eyes, his forehead as domed as a skull's. She saw an expression, if an expression at all, of total resolve, as if everything that he was—everything—was exposed in his skeletal face. He wore a dark suit, too small for him, that he might have been wearing for such occasions since he was a youth. He finally said, "Hilary," and she turned to him.

She asked, "Will you go to the reception at the Reform Club?"

"Yes," he answered. "Will you?"

"I'd thought I wouldn't, but if you go—"

"Then you'll come with me. We'll walk together."

The day, though gray, was warm, and as they were crossing Trafalgar Square Colin asked Hilary if she wouldn't mind stopping there before going on to the crowded reception.

She said she would do whatever he cared to do.

She stood by him as he studied one of the grand, gushing fountains, and she wondered what he saw in its majesty, what he saw in the majesty of Trafalgar Square, because the place was, she thought, majestic, or stopping here with Colin made her imagine it was, as if he had a deep appreciation she was aware of in him but that had never occurred to her before. The jets of water flashed in the gray light as with light of their own. She followed him when he went to a stone bench at the corner of the square, and they sat next to each other.

Hilary asked, "Do you know when women stopped wearing hats?"

He thought, his head lowered, then he lifted his head and said, "Odd, isn't it, that it hadn't occurred to me before you mentioned it this very moment that women don't wear hats the way they used to."

"So much does happen without our being aware."

"So much," he said. "You know, in the church, I was wondering whose idea it was to have a memorial service for Charlotte. She wouldn't have wanted one. She knew she wasn't important enough and would have considered it pretentious. Now everyone is given a memorial service. It's too absurd."

A tall Black man in a white kaftan came up to the fountain to study it for a long while, then he dipped a hand into the water in the basin before he left.

Hilary said, "I stopped seeing Charlotte when my parents died. Did you see much of her?"

"In the past, she came to stay at Elshieshields where my parents and I would spend holidays from London. I recall the first time she came, when I was a child. She exclaimed, seeing the house, 'My dear, crenellations, oh, this is going to be fun.' I was taught, rightly, to believe I wasn't important enough to consider myself superior to anyone else. She made me appreciate, because she had great appreciations of her own life, that my life was really rather special. I had never got that appreciation from my parents. After my parents died, she came to stay with me for a visit or two and always did make me aware of how special my life was. I saw less and less of her as the years passed, I don't know quite why, as you don't know quite why women stopped wearing hats. Perhaps she thought that my life—or, perhaps more to the point, her life—had ceased to be special. She withdrew totally when she knew she was dying."

"You knew she was dying?"

"I knew, but I knew more that she wouldn't want anyone to make a fuss about her dying. She herself made no fuss about dying, none at all."

"She would have thought the memorial service too much of a fuss?"

"She would have."

"I think I agree with that."

"I certainly want no fuss."

Great bright jets of water rose high from the fountain into the air, into which they seemed to disappear and from which they then fell.

He said, quietly, "Strange to say, I find myself more and more asking myself what is British."

Hilary tried to laugh. "Such as?"

Colin spoke in a quiet monotone, still staring at the fountain as if what he said was incidental to what he was looking at. "I was reading in the *Times Literary Supplement* a review of the collected works of a contemporary but very old German philosopher—I can't recall his name—who wrote something that struck me for being utterly non-British. What he wrote was, more or less, about the incomprehensibility of death."

"I don't understand," Hilary said.

She was somewhat surprised that Colin, whom she had never suspected of having an intellectual life, read the *Times Literary Supplement*, much less articles on German philosophers.

"I shouldn't think I do either," Colin said. "But, understanding or not, what I was made aware of is that to us British there is nothing incomprehensible about death, is there? That is a help to me, you know, a great help in dealing with the death of Jonathan."

"What is there to be made incomprehensible about it?" Hilary asked.

Moving only his eyes, Colin looked at her as if to confirm from her expression that she was serious. Hilary submitted to this scrutiny because Colin, knowing her as little as he really did, could only have had the past impression from her that she was not deeply serious.

He said, "Yes, I agree, yes, nothing is incomprehensible if we put our minds to it. Nevertheless, it's our limitation, I think, to believe there is nothing at all incomprehensible, in life or death, if only we put our minds to it."

"I would like to believe that."

"Well, I suppose we must believe it, or we're lost."

She had intimidated him. In his grief, he had wanted some meaning in Jonathan's death, and she had made him revert, as if it had been in him to revert to reasoning, to holding against any meaning in the incomprehensibility of death.

"Oh yes," Hilary said, "oh yes, blessedly yes, we would be lost."

Colin touched her knee, having, she felt, nothing more to say. "We'll go now."

But Hilary hadn't said what there was in her to say. "In a little, just a little."

"Just a little," Colin agreed.

It came to her why she hadn't been able to write to Colin. Really, her reaction to Jonathan's death was absurd. Stupidly, Hilary had, since his death, come to dislike Jonathan, a ghost intent on drawing Ted away from her and their lives together toward what Colin would call the incomprehensible. She would not, herself, be drawn into the incomprehensible, and she would not allow Ted to be, if she was able to hold back Ted from all that he was drawn to, drawn to, she thought, in a way that lately worried her. Because she knew from their past lives together his vulnerability to giving in to something in him he couldn't help, so much couldn't help that he lay on the floor and she stood over him and insisted, get up, and he got up. He had been incomprehensible to her at that past time, and she could not bear his again giving in to whatever he couldn't help. She had helped him, he often told her he had helped her, by not taking him seriously, by calling him *teddy bear*. And he liked that.

Abruptly, she said to Colin, "I'm so sorry about Jonathan."

"Thank you," he said.

She had become serious. She now wanted to say more about Jonathan's death, but she had said everything that, she knew, Colin wanted to hear. She noted that he appeared, for the very starkness of his looks, yes, noble.

Now Colin, held there by his thinking, didn't move from the bench. He raised and lowered his shoulders as if laughing, though no laughter came from him, just a slight heightening of his voice. "I recall my father telling me that a gentleman—a gentleman in Scotland, that is—never sits down to eat porridge at breakfast, but eats it with salt standing with his back to the fire or looking out of the window or at his barometer."

"Do you do that?"

"I don't ever have porridge now, but when I did, as a child, it was with brown sugar and cream." He again raised and lowered his shoulders, this time without levity. "But I shall have to begin eating it again, this time with salt, to remind myself that I am, after all—"

A breeze rose and made the spray of the water from the fountain shift to the side.

"Well," he said, "it doesn't matter."

"What?" Hilary asked.

And here Colin did laugh. He said, "After all, special."

"In being Scots?"

"Yes, I think so, in being Scots, in being who I am."

"What does that mean? I'm English, Welsh, Irish, and God-knows-what-else, perhaps even Scottish."

"It means that I am spending much more money than I can afford on repairing Elshieshields to make it truly habitable, and may have to sell London to get the job done properly," Colin said, and after a moment added, "We really should be going."

"Let's wait, just a little longer. I don't think I've ever truly talked with you about anything we might understand about each other."

"There is that."

But they sat in silence until Hilary said, "I think that Jessica and Ted share something between the two of them that I don't share with him."

"What could that be?"

"Dear, dear, Colin, nothing to be alarmed about, I'm sure of that. Could it be that they are both Americans?"

"I'm not quite sure what makes an American able to know what they could possibly share."

"And I, what could I possible say?" Hilary said. "To me, at least, they are strange, Americans are."

"Strange?"

"Because we assume that it is American to be ambitious and to fulfill all one's ambitions, no matter where an American is from in that huge American world. About which, really, we make generalizations we wouldn't tolerate in an American making a generalization about the British. But I dare say that, in general, Americans believe that America is fated."

"Fated?"

"That, for all that America promises, it will end in a disaster."

"Is that in Ted?"

"Yes, I think it is. He does take himself very seriously."

"I have never thought that about Jessica, if she takes herself very seriously. Perhaps she does. I have to admit I hardly think of her as American. But then, I also have to admit, I know her as my beloved wife."

They rose from the stone bench and walked through Trafalgar Square, among the fountains, to Pall Mall.

He all at once said, "My papa ate his porridge with salt."

"As you recall."

"As I recall. There was wine on the table only when there was a guest, one bottle. A boy, I recall a guest staring at the bottle while we were at soup, and I was embarrassed, but I knew my father held to the custom, no wine with soup."

"Was that a Scots custom?"

"It must have been, given my father. If a friend was invited, he was allowed to pour a little sherry into his soup, but he had to be rather an intimate friend."

Entering the Reform Club, where the reception was packed with people among whom women in black dresses held out serving trays of red and white wine or little sausages, Hilary and Colin remained together at the open double doorway, a little removed from the crowd inside.

Colin said, "As for incomprehension, I find Jessica's reaction to Jonathan's death totally incomprehensible. She is Catholic, but she is, after all, an American Catholic, and I suppose that makes a difference."

"As is Ted."

"Quite."

A woman came to them with a tray of glasses of wine. Both Hilary and Colin declined with little motions of their heads and the woman swerved away as if she had not been coming to them.

"How Catholic are you?" Hilary asked.

"Old Scots Catholic through my father," Colin answered. "My mother was in fact Welsh Methodist. My public school was Bryanston, which is meant to be Catholic, but is dominated, rather, by the Church of England. I boarded there not because it is Catholic, but because I wasn't clever enough for a top public school. My parents never did go much to church."

Alone, Hilary walked along Pall Mall, and, at Saint James's, decided to walk home. She thought she might not see Colin again, and that was all right. And it would be all right if she didn't see Jessica ever again. They seemed to her to belong in the past, too far in the past to have any reason to be present. She was present, now, in London, which was familiar to her, and she was reassured by the familiarity. She was always happy in London.

In Green Park, she stopped to look at the exotic ducks in the pond, and she asked herself, but why was she unhappy?

She wished that Ted were with her so that they would both look at the ducks, amused, both of them, by their exoticism, because she could amuse Ted. And he knew she could amuse him.

And she would bring him back from where he had gone in his own unhappiness to be, if not happy. Ted was never really happy, and perhaps had never been, but she had made him, and she could still make him, as pleased with life as he was when with her and she was, herself, pleased to be with him.

And yet, she felt that something had happened to him that made it very difficult to bring him back, and she thought, really, she no longer had the will, which he so counted on in her—the will, or, better, the spirit to make him spirited by not taking him seriously. He did not want her to take him seriously.

If the death of Jonathan had once been the cause, that cause now appeared to her so far in the past that other causes, from she had no idea where, had to have occurred. Or they had occurred to him from before she had met him, introduced to her in the foyer of the Sloane Square Theatre during an intermission by an American she had known but since had lost contact with. She had remained in contact with Ted—her handsome, lively Ted Beauchemin, whose face kept changing with vivid expression, the most vivid a look of wonder at everything she said, as though he had never before met anyone like her, his wonder so wonderful to her. And, oh, that first night together in her bed, now their bed! That first night of sleeping with him after the letting go! And those times when he returned home from business away, especially in the early morning when she was still asleep and he came into the room and woke her and she watched him quickly undress and she lifted the bed clothes for him to come in to her, with a slight smell of his body, and hold her! No, that she could not, would not, give up, not for any cause that denied her the happiness of what she had with him.

She sat on a bench at one end. At the other end was an old man, a man, she imagined, from a London that no longer existed, because he was wearing a black pinstriped three-piece suit and held a tightly furled umbrella at an angle between his knees, and his plain, dark tie was tightly knotted, and he looked, himself, to be tightly composed. He had a white, stiff moustache. Hilary glanced at him when she sat, and just then he looked at her and nodded, and she nodded back.

"Lovely day," he said.

"Lovely," she said, and she waited. In fact, the sky was overcast.

He said, "It gives me such a sense of privilege to be out in the park when the day is so lovely."

"Oh, yes," Hilary responded.

"You feel the same?"

"I do, I do."

"Well, you see," the old man said, "I always take an umbrella with me just in case."

"I should think that's always wise."

"One never knows."

"Oh, indeed, one doesn't."

What a pleasure, Hilary thought, to have this little conversation as if in a language that was extinct.

She lived in London, she loved London, and however much she knew that London was changing, there were the vestiges of a past London that survived the changes, and this was a London, not of nostalgia, no, but a London of people who did love London, and had their markings, who could say, "Not south of the Thames," as if that exclusion made Kensington the acceptable edge of where to live. Or could say, "No brown in town," as if to wear a brown greatcoat in London were not acceptable, with some amusement at the foreigner who didn't know. And there was the expression, Milk in First, M.I.F., which placed a class of people who poured milk into their cups before the tea—many, many references to outdated manners and words, but which sustained the markings of a London that was disappearing, but which she held to.

She liked to think she was not politically con-
servative, and, when it came to voting, she would
always vote for Labour, and she would then leave
the outcome of the vote to whatever rises in taxes
that meant.

Well, London was itself, and whenever she
gave a drinks party she knew that almost everyone knew one another, and would, standing
about with glasses of white wine and someone
hired to pass around the little sausages on a silver dish, agree that changes were inevitable. And
she liked this duplicity, if that is what it was, of
her drawing room with its antique yellow tea set
on a bamboo table behind a screen pasted with
images cut out from magazines of a London, of
an England, of a United Kingdom, that no longer
held against the changes, which everyone agreed
were inevitable.

And there was this, long gone, she thought
never to start a message on a postcard with the
salutation "dear," and always end it with an illeg-
ible squiggle.

The old man said, "My wife died quite unex-
pectedly, and now I wait, with some expectation,
for my death."

And Hilary thought, Only someone who
didn't know London would assume that the
British were so reticent about their private lives

that there could be no openness towards another, even in a public park.

Hilary said, "As for that, I've just come from a memorial service."

"You see," the man said.

"Yes, I see."

"May I ask for whom?"

Hilary graciously gave the name, and the old man frowned, as though trying to recollect, then said, "I didn't know her, but why should I have?"

"One never knows, you might have passed her walking through the park and noted her hat." Hilary laughed.

The old man laughed. "That would have been quite a while ago, but I do remember women's hats, some with quite shameless feathers on them."

"That had to have been a very, very long time ago."

"Well, you see, I am very old, very. And if I tell you I am just past one hundred years old, you may look at me with surprise that I was there to witness women with big hats and am still alive"

Shocked to hear that the man was as old as he claimed, Hilary said, "My mother once told me that she and my father were invited to a royal garden party at Buckingham Palace, and my mother, who was, I suppose, rather liberal in her views, didn't wear a hat, and she and my father were not invited again."

"Well, good on her, because, you know, those garden parties are very boring—manufactured sandwiches and plastic cups of tea under tents, and the royals guided by courtiers to those, among the massive crowd, who might be of any interest. Poor royals having to sustain interest in people they have no interest in. Shall I tell you a story?"

"Please do."

"My wife and I were once invited to Balmoral, and at dinner, one of the young royals said, If I have to open another power station, or something such, I shall scream, and the Queen Mother Elizabeth said, 'We love to open power stations.' And, you know, I was moved. I had, for all my received ideas, thought the royals would be someone staid, you know, but no, not a bit of it, they were having a good time, and I did my best to join in, and I swear, my feeling was that anyone there, however unknown to them, could have joined in the fun. Oh, I did, I did have fun."

"That must be a happy memory," Hilary said.

"I have a vivid memory, I do, I do, and I should like to tell you that I have been very happy, very, and I live now on that happiness."

The man blurred in Hilary's vision of him.

She said, "You can't know how that helps me."

"Then I can count myself privileged again to have been of help to a delightful woman I have happened to sit with on a park bench."

And then, in her blurred vision, he was gone.

Hilary pressed the tears from her eyes with her thumbs, thinking, Here I am, and it is all so familiar and all so strange. She was so glad to have had a momentary vision of a Great Britain that had ceased to be, and, yes, she would hold onto that moment, however irrelevant it was to her daily life and to the tomorrows that would come to her with Ted.

Not to take ourselves too seriously, she thought, to be British in the way she wanted was not to take oneself too seriously.

And because she was thinking about herself as British, in whatever way she was British, didn't the old gentleman she had just spoken to represent a Britain that should not be taken too seriously, but with, oh, some lightness of irony?

Because, she thought, irony was the saving grace of, well, Westminster and her interest in politics, which she never was able to discuss with Ted because he was without politics. But she was invited by a friend from the Labour back benches to the public gallery, an advantage she sometimes pressed on him, and sat looking down at the House of Commons with the wonder of a debate in the chamber where the role of the Speaker was to shout *order! order!* to the roar of House, which to her counted as an entertainment, if irony was an entertainment.

And so, the prime minister would address Mr. Speaker, who might stop the prime minister with a point of order, and the prime minister would have to sit until the Speaker permitted him to continue, and the prime minister would stand and again place his papers on the dispatch box and address Mr. Speaker, who represented the most disinterested principles in the House of Commons, and who was the most entertaining person present, shouting *order! order!* to a House in roaring disorder as the prime minister addressed him, Mr. Speaker, not the members of parliament. How could one not bring to the government the levity of some irony, though this was, yes, where government was made, but where the Speaker tried to make government obey *order! order!* as if government was always in disorder and over and over needed the Speaker to shout *order! order!* which, however, was not kept for long.

This sense of irony saved her marriage with Ted, toward whom she was able to sustain her sometimes too clever spirit, and if that was the too clever spirit of a Londoner, she was a Londoner, amused to hear her friend from the back benches of the Labour Party joke at a drinks party about one of his constituents. Ted did not understand.

There was irony in her thinking of the gentleman she had sat next to on the park bench. She had been amused by him and his umbrella. How else but with a degree of levity could she remember that cultured but slightly ridiculous man? He was there in a world she was born into and, though it was leaving her day by day, she hadn't altogether left.

And, oh, how could one think of the Queen and the world she sustained without some faint irony, the world in which a woman always carried a purse by its strap over an arm and always, always wore a hat, always in the same style, but always a new hat every time she appeared in public, which meant hundreds and hundreds and hundreds of hats worn once and never again.

And Ted? Oh, Ted, when it all came to Ted, he was a man without irony, totally without irony.

Twenty-three

The morning Ted was to go to Helsinki, he was made redundant, let go. A security guard checked that Ted didn't take away what belonged to the company as he cleared out his desk, and this humiliation made Ted appear, in his own eyes, minuscule in his chair. If he had thought of taking any company property away, such as files containing documents and annual reports and company descriptions, he would have done so the day before, when he'd been awakened to the possibility of his being made redundant. But he had been as if asleep. And even if awake, he would not have taken anything that did not belong to him, mostly because he would have looked at the files on his desk as no longer having anything to do with his life.

Under the eyes of the security guard, he filled his briefcase with such items as he'd found useful to have at hand during the often fourteen-hour days he put in at work— aspirin, toothbrush and paste, eye drops, clean socks, a tie (an abandoned tie with a paisley design he, aware as he had been made of what was right and what was wrong in dress, had quickly recognized was infra dig), an alarm clock, even a small sewing kit, a framed photograph of himself and Hilary. And when he reached for a file of his own personal papers on his desk, the guard asked to examine it. He was not allowed to take with him the old material left from his training course from years before, and each of the books in the shelves by his desk were scrutinized as to whether or not they had been bought on the company account, even the expensive picture books about the cities Ted had been to and bought for himself. He left all the books.

As he approached home, he saw Hilary standing at the window of the sitting room, her figure flat against the sunlight except for some loose, brilliant strands of her hair. Turning to him, she said, "Strange, I've been looking out of the window, and I didn't see you approaching the house."

He said, in a low voice, "Then I've suddenly appeared."

"You have that ability?"

"All you have to do is call out my name."

She said, "Ted."

He encircled his arms about her but kept his face at a distance as he looked at her mouth, her cheeks, her chin, her brow, her eyes, and held back with a more and more subtle tension between them, then he slowly rotated his face close to hers as if to see her all together, and then kissed her, gently kissed her face all over, again and again and again.

He leaned his forehead against hers and said, "Here I am."

But he felt he wasn't there, that he was trying to reassure her of his presence with her, though he was somewhere else, and she sensed this because she eased herself away from him with a smile and moved toward the doorway into the hall, as if she had a reason to go, but at the doorway she stopped and asked, "Would you like tea?"

"I'll get it."

"I will."

"Let me," he insisted.

Hilary fell onto the middle of the sofa, which was in shadows. "Thank you," she said.

Ted went down to the kitchen to prepare tea, and while he did, that other Ted stayed close by him, watching him warm the pot, spoon in just the right amount of tea, make sure the water was boiling before he poured it out, as Hilary had taught him. Putting the pot and cups and saucers and little jug of milk on a tray, he thought he now depended on that other Ted watching him, waiting for what he might say or do. He more than depended on this other Ted's anticipation of what he might say or do. He felt an exhilaration in the attention of that other Ted. The tray was on the table, lying at a slight angle on the disordered papers that were always there. He picked up the tray to go upstairs.

Ted placed his cup on the coffee table and he rested his head on the back of the armchair, and looking upward he said in a tired, light voice, "I was once in Seattle, from where, after a meeting, I was supposed to go to São Paulo, Brazil. But there was such a thunderstorm, the airplane was rerouted to St. Louis, where we were put up for the night. I expected to fly to Miami in the morning, but when I woke up early, I found out that the storm was raging across the whole of the Midwest and that all flights out of St. Louis were cancelled. I hired a driver to take me to Memphis—a seven-hour drive, from the north to the cotton fields of the South—because I thought Memphis would be out of range of the storm and I would be able to fly out from there. I'd never been. The Mississippi River divides the city, effectively divides the rich whites from the poor Blacks. The airport is on the Black side. I passed through slums that were as bad as any I'd seen in Black Africa, right in America."

Hilary asked, "Did you get to São Paulo?"

"I did."

"You've seen more of the world than I have."

"More than I've wanted to see. Sometimes I wonder why I've collected the maps I have from all the places I've been to on business trips, as if my being there were an accomplishment beyond being there for meetings. I suppose I had the ambition, which was a part of my job, of going everywhere, everywhere on the globe, to be able to say I'd been there. I wanted to go to the remotest places, and I did go, even to Africa. I thought, I really thought, that if the world had only itself to depend on to make itself whole, what I was doing was essential to the world's wholeness. Like some mad missionary, I believed that everyone in this world—everyone, all over the world—could connect, so that even a cup, a pencil, a bar of soap would be seen to connect everyone, the whole world, in one."

"And diamonds and gold?" Hilary asked.

Ted closed his eyes.

Hilary said, "You once went to Africa? I didn't know."

His eyes closed, Ted said, "I went to investigate a request for investment in a logging operation in a rainforest. The request was turned down, as we knew it would be, but we thought we should have a look. But of course, Malaysian and Chinese companies have no doubt made deals, and the rainforest will be devastated."

"You didn't bring back a map from Africa."

Ted opened his eyes. "No, I left that out."

"Have you left other places out?"

Ted shrugged.

"You won't tell me?"

"I'm sorry."

"Why?"

"Oh, places where I thought nothing would help, and certainly not investing in them, some of them places of horror."

He looked at the coffee table with piles of books and magazines and among them the tray with the teapot and the cups, and beyond them he looked at Hilary.

He said, "If you were asked to go to Africa to do whatever you could to help, you would go. You're that generous."

"I'm sorry, I'd have to disappoint you," she said, "because not only the horrors of Africa but of all the world are too much for me to get on with even preparing a meal."

"You're generous with me."

She said quietly, "You're home at an odd hour. Were you made redundant?"

"I was."

He rose from the armchair and around the coffee table and sat by her on the sofa. He leaned toward her and pressed his forehead against her shoulder.

She said, "I think I can help you find a position in another bank."

"I've made enough contacts to seek out some work."

Hilary said, "One of your shoelaces is untied."

He leaned far over to tie the shoelace, and then he picked up one of the cushions and placed it behind his head and rested against it, and as if about to fall asleep, he said, "Now my shoelace is tied."

"I truly would do anything I could to make you laugh a little."

"Thanks," Ted said quietly.

As quietly, Hilary said, "I'm sorry. Of course you're not up to laughing."

"No," he said, "not now."

She said, "I met Colin earlier at a memorial service. After, we sat in Trafalgar Square and we talked. It was an interesting talk, somewhat about death. He said something that I can't recall, but, yes, it was interesting, and surprising because I hadn't thought Colin had intellectual interests. When I left him at the Reform Club, I thought, really, that he is of some nobility, as unassuming as he is."

"Who was the memorial for?"

"An old friend of my parents. You wouldn't have known her."

"I suppose I wouldn't have."

"I do hope you're not implying, again, that you don't really belong in my world."

"No, I'm not implying. The fact is that I don't."

"I wonder where you feel you do belong."

"You know that I do adapt, wherever I am."

"And then withdrawing into yourself, as if you were entirely alone."

"That's as I am."

"As you are."

Ted suddenly raised his head from the cushion and Hilary withdrew her head from his shoulder.

He asked, "You won't give up on me, will you?"

"Give up on you? Whatever made you imagine that I would? Have I ever made you suspect I might?"

"Well, given how much I fail, how do you put up with me?"

"I'm not sure how, but I do."

Ted lifted her hand and kissed it, and then held it in his.

She said, "You never talk about your parents."

"Don't I?"

"Not much."

"I didn't much visit them, did I?"

"You weren't close to them."

"They were close to each other, I know. My mother helped my father a lot, morally and spiritually, when he went bankrupt. She did that for him."

"And you, didn't they do a lot for you?"

"Maybe they tried, but I always felt I was in a different world from them."

"Your world is so different?"

"I like to think it is, I like to think I've come far—far enough, anyway, to be here with you."

Hilary said, "I'd like to go out into the garden. Come with me. The sunlight is mellow now."

But as she left, he remained as he had been.

He thought he understood her irony, that she always treated him with the irony of never quite believing in what he said or did, so there was in her thinking about him a low level of not taking him seriously. Her voice in his mind sounded with a little, joking lilt to it. She would even think he was not to be taken seriously if he told her that what he most wanted, what that Ted looming above him most wanted for him, if it were possible to say what that looming Ted wanted. Hilary would make him feel he was a little bit of a fool for such thoughts.

He was a big fool.

He knew that if he ever tried to talk to Hilary in a way that he, himself, considered as serious as he could be, Hilary would simply smile and run a hand through his hair and ask him if he wanted a cup of tea, and that she would treat him as a boy, would at least relieve him of his pretension as a serious man, because the pretensions of a boy were to be treated lightly, as Hilary always did.

And he could rise to her level of light-spiritedness, he could, he had been able to, and he could again. That was one of the reasons why Hilary had liked being with him when they had been dating. He made her laugh even if he didn't quite see what in him made her laugh. She would say, "You are so funny." And he liked that. He liked making her laugh, he liked being funny for her.

Twenty-four

On the platform of the Baker Street Station, Jessica heard an announcement over the loudspeaker that trains would be delayed due to an illness far out on the Bakerloo Line. She would have to wait.

It occurred to her that the announcement on the loudspeaker of someone, on some distant line, who had taken ill, was a euphemism for someone having thrown himself into the way of an oncoming train—a suicide. And if, when in the past she had heard the announcement, she'd felt a pang, now she thought, as though in retrospect, that it was very wrong for someone to put all of London at the mercy of such an act, a social crime. And she wondered at how this objection to anyone acting on the impulse to commit suicide came to her now in her always shifting thoughts and feelings. She really was too slight to make them consistent.

There was no way, no way at all, that Lady Kerr would commit suicide, or even to imagine how she would commit it. The act of pushing through the others and throwing herself off the platform onto a train rushing into the station would have been as absurd, she thought, as the past possibility of confiding in Ted that she would do it. She had once wanted to confide this in Ted, but she hadn't, and she was relieved that she hadn't.

She had once heard of a person, saved from the attempt, recounting that in the seconds before it would, it seemed, inevitably happen, the sense occurred overwhelmingly: *I don't want to die.*

No, no, I don't want to die.

Still, what she had to live for was very little, it seemed to her. It was everything Colin had to offer her, and that, now, was a life in stark Scotland, where the view from the sitting room window, usually through rain, was of Scots pines and ravens. And it was highly unlikely that she would be able to set up a gift shop because she herself knew almost nothing about tartans, and she wasn't interested enough to learn if, in fact, she had the permission to sell them.

She thought of walking with Colin in the Scottish countryside along a river in which sheep had drowned, their bodies rotting in the hard, dark current, because it did happen that stray sheep fell into streams in Scotland and were drowned, and they rotted there.

The wait was not as long as she had expected. Perhaps the person who had attempted to throw himself onto the tracks was held back; or perhaps the driver of the train, always alert to such happenings, had stopped in time.

The doors of the train slid open, and Jessica, among others, entered the carriage, and, standing, swayed with them until a young man, a handsome young man sitting before her, rose to offer her his seat, and, lightly thanking him, she sat. He wore a red kerchief tied tightly about his smooth neck.

No, it had not been a mistake for her to have married Colin. He could be quietly amusing, as when he came into the kitchen, where she happened to be, with eggs from his hens and his comment that the cock of the roost seemed very pleased with himself. When they were invited out to dinner, he would bring along a gift of six eggs wrapped in newspaper, and this always charmed his friends. He was a charming man.

Well, the foxes put an end to that.

At Elshieshields, he had his library in the tower where he did spend a lot of time, and where, the fire lit, they would have afternoon tea, but where, otherwise, he shut the door to her, in what she considered a gentle way, because he gently preferred to be on his own part of the day.

And he was so well read, and had such a good memory, that he could quote a Victorian poet about a very old door handle on a heavy, nail-studded door on the outside of the tow-er. Inserted into the handle was a length of iron forged into a long twist, and around this long twist of iron was an iron ring to rasp up and down the iron for long dead visitors to announce themselves. It was called tirling at the pin. She truly admired Colin for his erudition, and she was, slowly, reading the Elizabethan poets.

One short sleep past, we wake eternally.

Oh yes.

What to do with such a belief if one did not believe? To read the poem for the masterly use of all the basic elements in poetry, from which all less mastery wasn't really poetry? Was that enough? To read the poem as a structured ex-pression of a past belief, an historical reassurance that such a belief had once been possible, was that enough?

Life eternal.

The train stalled in the dark tunnel and for a moment the lights went out, then flickered, then came on, and the train jolted a little, then on.

Jessica looked up at the young man, who moved his shoulders as if in rhythm with the movement of the train.

And Death, thou shalt die.

The young man standing above her was looking down at her, the young man, the handsome young man wearing a red handkerchief tied tightly about his neck. He smiled at her, a friendly smile, and she smiled back, a friendly smile, and she looked away.

Soul's delivery.

If she couldn't look up at the young man's face for his expression, she saw he changed his weight from foot to foot as if barely suppressing the dancing that was happening within him.

How wonderful it would be to use the words, freely, as though it mattered: the great, the grand, the sublime.

She looked up again at the face of the young man. He was not looking at her, but his face was filled with enough expression of enchantment for her continued attention, and she went on looking at him for as long as his eyes were somewhere else. But he glanced down at her and caught her looking up at him, so there she was, herself, caught, and all she could do was smile and ask, "Are you a dancer?"

He smiled. "Only when something comes over me."

"When is that?"

He laughed and said, "Whenever I'm on my way to see my girlfriend."

Jessica laughed too, a quiet laugh. "I'm happy for you."

"Thanks."

She said, to let go of him, "I'll let you go on dancing."

Again, he said, "Thanks," but he had become self-conscious and was still.

The train stopped at Saint John's Wood station, and the young man moved aside to let Jessica pass him; as she did, she raised a hand and nodded, and he did the same back to her. She was so sorry she had embarrassed him so he had stopped making dance movements, but no doubt he had continued, within himself. She wished she had said to him, Have a happy time with your girlfriend, but she was standing at the doors, which were sliding open. She left the train, the doors slid shut and sped into the darkness of the tunnel, the young man on his way to his girlfriend.

So thy love may be my love's sphere.

From the Saint John's Wood Tube station, she went round a corner to a shop to buy for breakfast the next morning, when Colin would be back from Scotland. Colin liked grilled kippers for breakfast. And grilled tomatoes and mushrooms. But not porridge.

Oh no, she thought, no, no, she did not want to die.

As she was paying for the kippers, wrapped in paper, she thought of the dancing young man on the Tube, and she kept her hand out, even though she held the change that'd been given to her, so the shopkeeper asked, "Lady Kerr?"

But she remained with her hand held out. Then she said, "I am sorry," and brought her hand away, and it seemed to her that all her actions were delayed by the sudden love she felt for that young man dancing on the train. She carried her purchases home, and with her key in the lock of the front door, she thought, I love someone I don't know, whom I will never see again, who will forget me when he is with his girlfriend, and who will die.

So in a voice, so in a shapeless flame.

Now, putting her shopping in the refrigerator—the kippers, the tomatoes and mushrooms, the bottle of milk and the butter, and, having seen them at the greengrocer's as the first of the season, the ripe plums—the remembered lines came to her written by someone else, someone she didn't know. She shut the refrigerator door.

How one was made aware of ordinary acts that somehow became extraordinary, such as making a pot of tea and, putting all the tea things on a tray, going up to the study, which always appeared to be greenish in the light from the windows. She sat at the desk, where there was a telephone.

She wouldn't ring Ted. No, she would let him go. There was so much she had to let go, but she would do it, perhaps with a sense of accomplishment simply in letting it go. And, yes, she did feel some sense of accomplishment in letting Ted go. She poured out tea into a cup and took a sip, but the tea was too hot, and she placed the cup carefully back on the saucer. Her elbow poised on the edge of the desk, she placed a hand over her forehead.

Love must not be, but take a body too.

She rang Colin. She said, in a bright voice, "I bought you smoked kippers for your breakfast tomorrow morning. Don't be late for the train."

And he said, in a voice that was bright for him, "I'll collect you at the station."

The young man on the underground train, the one wearing a red bandana tied about his neck, on his way to his girlfriend, dancing on his way—why, thinking about him, shouldn't she be light-spirited? Why shouldn't she imagine with a lightness of spirit the young man meeting his girlfriend and his holding her in his arms?

Yes, she could be a little spirited. And that little spirit was her love for the young man with the red bandana, a tender love, for the young man, for everyone, because why shouldn't she feel tender love for everyone, tender love because everyone would die?

Oh, Ted.

Something had passed between them. She had felt it and she was sure he had felt it, but it was impossible to say what that was, because it was no more than a great letting go, a great sense of freedom that came, not from them, no, not from them, but from far outside, as though from a great windy space. And there was nothing to be said about letting everything go in that great windy space. It was not belief, no, not any more belief than poetry required belief to be written, from beyond belief.

She was staring at the magnifying glass on the desk with a deer's antler for a handle, and it came to her that she was, in fact, calm, calm in the midst of all her thinking. She was calm because she had fallen in love with the young man on the train, who knew nothing about her, nothing about Jonathan, nothing about Colin and nothing about Ted, about Hilary, about anyone in her life, and nothing about her. Because she didn't know anything about him but that he was on his way, dancing in his soul, to meet his lady, her love was impersonal. And because he knew nothing about her, the love was all in the great, grand sublime.

She picked up the magnifying glass and, looking through it, magnified the things on the desk, the cup of tea and the saucer, a red leather pen holder, a red leather-bound address book, a letter opener, a paper clip, a black button that was still threaded with a length of red cotton.

She would give a drinks party, the last in the house before the move to Scotland, and then she would leave London behind. She was calm enough not to mind; she was calm enough that she didn't mind much about anything else but the thought about giving a drinks party. Yes, a drinks party, and she would make a point of inviting the African couple, as a reassurance of their inclusion in her and Colin's world. And, really, she wasn't sure she would like to include them, not knowing how they had become so rich and honored for their loyalty to the Crown, but she would do what she supposed she should do and invite them. Supposed, she thought, because she was still American enough to be impressed by honors bestowed by the Crown, and at the same time British enough to wonder if there were reasons enough for them to be in prison, given the diamond broach the woman wore.

It occurred to her. Would she invite Ted, Ted and Hilary? The question surprised her because she would of course invite them.

She did not want to die.

Winding a length of red cotton from the spool around her index finger, she began to make a list of people she would invite, and then she stared at the cotton about her finger and wondered how the spool had appeared on her desk.

As the title of a poem, this occurred to her: a spool of red cotton.

She heard herself say, "The spool of red cotton."

Twenty-five

At the bay window, Ted looked out at the empty street in the light from a streetlamp. Someone walked past the house—a man, an old man carrying a small suitcase, and the sight of an old man at night carrying a suitcase shocked Ted, so he drew back.

In the dark, he found his way up the stairs and to the landing off the bedroom, where he switched on a light, all the light he needed to see into their bedroom, where Hilary, he assumed, was now asleep. In the light from the landing, he passed the bureau on which Hilary heaped her jewelry. On the heap, he noted a gold bracelet with the little diamond he had bought her at a high moment of extravagance. Hilary tried to confine her messiness to small areas, such as this bureau, on which, besides the jewelry, were make-up compacts, little square and round boxes, and, incongruously, a fork on a plate.

After switching off the light on the landing, in the darkness of the bedroom he bumped into the bottom of the bed, but Hilary did not respond. He felt his way under the covers and lay still beside her.

No, no, he told himself, he would not give into the longing of the other Ted, the longing that that other Ted held him in the thrall of, the thrall of what could never be. He wouldn't give in to that, but would fight for the Ted he was, the Ted he was with Hilary, whom he believed he loved, loved for the life she gave him, for all the tender pleasures of love.

His panic was that he may have already lost Hilary, and he, Ted, the Ted who loved Hilary, had to reassure her of his love, had to reassure her in the simplest ways of everything that kept him in her world.

To lie with her in their warm bed, to remain awake when she fell asleep next to him, to think how safe we are here, how much in love. To feel her body beneath the loose shift she wore as a nightgown, the shift sometimes twisting about her when she moved in his arms.

Sustain this, he thought, sustain this.

The vision came to him of his parents in their bed, perhaps in each other's arms, a vision that occurred within the darkness of the bedroom where he and Hilary lay in their bed, and it seemed to him that his thinking rose up with the vision.

There was that strange separation between his parents in their early married life, from either side of which they had written letters of longing. Maybe he could have asked a relative, the sister of his mother, what had caused the separation, but after their deaths, one so soon after the other that their wakes and funerals seemed to have been one, he had wanted to return to Hilary quickly, and had only seen his aunt for coffee in her home. He could have asked her, and maybe she would have known something, but he hadn't, and he had thrown the letters away, having read only fragments. He hadn't wanted to know. And maybe the explanation was only that one of them was ill, or that one of them had had a severe breakdown. His mother, most likely, because she was a frail woman, a frail and gentle woman, an innocent woman. His father was always attentive to what she could not bear, which Ted did recall from moments when his father would see his mother standing very still and silent, as if waiting, and his father would go to her and hold her for a long while. And, because of her breakdown, it was thought that they should be separated for a while. Maybe a breakdown caused by the marriage that she had not been able to bear, maybe a miscarriage that caused in her a breakdown so she had had to recover in a sanitarium. His mother in a sanitarium? Again, he didn't want to know. All he knew from what he had read of their letters was everything that he wanted to know. And what he most knew was, when they came together, the longing they had both cried out to each other over the great space of their separation was fulfilled in him, in his birth, in Theodore Beauchemin.

And that should have been enough for him to stand against the other Ted. That should have been enough for him to believe that that Ted was dead. He was dead, he was, but that past Ted called on the present Ted from the dead, from where that Ted was with his dead parents. That old Ted wanted to reach out to the young Ted and take him into his arms as though taking up an innocent boy—to bring him, with the greatest love the living Ted had ever known, into the dark. That old Ted loved the young Ted, and wanted to save him.

He turned to Hilary and shifted close to her and placed an arm over her waist.

Hilary stretched out under the bedclothes and she held out her arms to Ted.

"Let's sleep," she said.

She slept and awoke to the absence of Ted beside her in the bed. Because of the heat, the curtains were drawn back, the window open, and light from the full moon, in the central pane of the top half of the many-paned window, shone into the room. She saw Ted standing against that light.

She was frightened of him, which she had never imagined being, never of Ted. The twisted sheet held against her breasts, she didn't move. A greater shock of alarm coursed through her when he, wearing only the t-shirt he slept in, walked out of the moonlight into the shadows at the bottom of their bed and stood there, facing her. She drew the sheet up closer about her shoulders and said, quietly, "Come to bed," and he walked slowly round to his side. She held the sheet up for him to get under it; it floated in the air for a moment and then fell loosely over them both.

As if he were not by her, but far, and she had to call him back, she said, in a low voice, "Ted," and he was still until she said, again, "Ted," and he turned to her, so they faced each other, his expression one of wondering why she had called him. Her voice even lower, she said, "I'm not going to ask you what's wrong, because I know you wouldn't be able to say."

"I wouldn't be able to say."

With a finger, she seemed to draw his face in the air, his forehead, his eyebrows, around his open eyes, his nose, his cheeks, his mouth, his chin.

She said, "I wish I could show you how much I love you, so that you'd believe at least in my love."

"You really like to think I'm funny, funny Ted."

Hilary drew herself close and pressed all her body against all of his. "How can you think that about someone I love so much?"

"I'm sorry."

"You know I'm not good at explaining myself, explaining anything. You know how I love to make love with you, and, oh, I feel you do with me, and that's a lot, that's a world to us both. But there's more, there's so much more, there really is another world of our love for each other. You've got to believe that. I honestly feel I wouldn't want to go on living if I thought you didn't believe that."

"I believe that."

Letting her arms hang loosely at his sides, she said, as a matter of fact, "But, I know it's not enough."

He pulled away from her arms and he lay flat on his back. She saw that his eyes were open and that his chest was heaving with his breathing.

She asked, "What, really, do you want, Ted, that I can't give you?"

He said, "You tell me."

"You know I can't."

"Well, I suppose no one can."

"Are you so upset by losing your job that you can't sleep?"

"I'd almost forgotten."

"Try to sleep."

"I'll try."

She said, "I'll tell you what we'll do. We'll go on a holiday, we'll leave London for a while, long enough for us to talk about what comes next for you. If you can't truly believe in my love for you, you've got to believe that something is promised. That's everything."

"I know."

"Ted, please take me seriously. I know you think that I don't, that I'm always too light with you and all your thoughts and feelings. But now I want you to listen to me seriously. We're young. I'm young enough to have a baby. I feel we should have a baby to fill our lives. After all, what greater promise in life can there be except a baby to nurture, to bring up, to love? Are you listening to me?"

"I'm listening."

"I don't feel you are."

"I am."

"Then what do you feel?"

"About what?"

"Having a baby?

"A baby? In this world?"

"Not in any other," Hilary said. "This world."

He appeared to sink away, but then, suddenly, he appeared to rise, and he said, "What I wanted was for Jonathan to die. That's what I wanted. What I want is for the world to end, that's what I want. I want the world to end in a massive, blazing, magnificent end. And these are my great sins."

"Ted," Hilary called, because he was far from her. "Ted," she called again.

Perhaps he was asleep, perhaps he was dreaming, and he spoke from his dream. This had never happened before. She felt that it would all go on happening, what hadn't happened before. And how could she stop it? It was all happening, and to the degree that she couldn't help it all happening, she was frightened. It was not in Hilary to be frightened, and least of all by Ted.

Ted fell back and pulled up the sheet to cover his head. Though she was unable to sleep, he turned away from her and suddenly became so still she thought he did fall asleep.

Her mind flashed with incoherent thoughts, as if they were visible flashes that revealed here a hand, there a foot, elsewhere a shoulder, an incoherent body.

She and Ted would go away for a while, she would think where, even though she didn't want to go because she had such a sense of fatality in their going.

No, no, she wouldn't let any sense of fatality come to her, and that the word occurred to her was only because it occurred, as so many words did that had almost nothing to do with her feelings. And yet the word occurred to her, and it did rouse in her some feeling, and, lying awake, she thought of blackberries, plums, peaches, apricots, apples, pears, grapes, in the order of their ripening. And what about kumquats, persimmons, pomegranates, whose seasons were strange to her?

When she showed delight at the Arab greengrocer about a fruit that she had not seen before, crushed together like sweets in a wooden box and each fruit wrapped in colored tissue, purplish and its peel as if shriveled, he told her they came from Lebanon, and he also told her the name, which she had forgot, and the box of fresh dates came from Egypt.

When she woke and saw the bed beside her was empty, the sheet thrown back, she sat up. Ted was at the window, the pre-dawn light now showing on the panes. She saw him raise the sash wide, for, she thought, more air, and seeing him sit on the windowsill she thought this, too, was for the cool coming in through the window. But when he raised his legs and, raising them, turned sideways so he was sitting on the sill, she jumped out of bed to rush to him and reached out to pull him towards her so he fell awkwardly onto her, and she held him steady in her arms, held him closely to her for her to save him, and, her face pressed into the side of his neck, she pleaded with him, "Oh, my love, oh, my love, oh my love," and felt his body give way to her in her arms.

Twenty-six

Ted beside her, Hilary drove though fields of tobacco, the large leaves on high stalks wilted in the sunshine, and here and there in the midst of the rows were small, prefabricated buildings without windows.

She knew that the tobacco was grown here in Italy because of sanctions against Rhodesian, or now Zimbabwean, tobacco, sanctions once meant to keep the British colony within the Commonwealth.

Old, stone tobacco drying towers had been left to fall apart in once abandoned fields, all from a past time when Rhodesian tobacco had replaced Italian tobacco. And now, Africans—dispossessed Africans—were hoeing the rows, here in Umbria, in Italy. Beyond the fields of tobacco appeared high-rise, cement apartment buildings with laundry on their little balconies, then, closer to town, sheep appeared in the dirt streets among the high-rises. Hilary followed a pickup truck into town.

She often glanced to the side to see Ted, Ted staring, wide-eyed and without expression, out onto the world.

The town was crowded for market day, and Hilary had to drive round and round the one-way streets to find a parking space, almost outside the town. They were unable to find a restaurant with a free table for lunch. They ate their sandwiches standing. Around them, some large Black African young men were speaking in their language and laughing. But one young African, his round face almost blue-black, was standing alone, leaning against a wall, not eating. His intelligent eyes were clear. Hilary saw his chest heave with a deep sigh, broad and muscular beneath his dirty t-shirt, and she noted that hanging by a thong about his neck was a little, triangular locket in which she knew was kept a fragment of the Koran.

Ted was leaning on a wall eating his panino and looking around in a distracted way, this distraction a worry to Hilary, for he appeared to be on a far edge of the world and only at moments aware of it, as when the green bottle of mineral water on the counter appeared to hold his attention, long enough for him to wonder at it, and then Ted appeared to stare at nothing. She was apprehensive about this stay in Italy, and she was apprehensive about Ted himself, as if he might do something that she could not imagine, because it was beyond her to imagine, as was anyone who wanted to die.

Leaving the shop with Ted, Hilary looked again at the young, powerful African, wanting to make him see that she saw him, so she looked at him with the need to approach him and, for just an instant, lay her head against his chest.

"Please tell me that you are fine," Hilary said to Ted.

"I am fine."

"I don't think you are."

"I am."

And he perhaps was, if a state of distraction was fine, though Hilary had to warn him not to trip over a rack of green bottles in the cobbled street that he seemed not to have seen.

She drove fast out of the town and into the hills, and beyond the hills into the mountains, eager to get where she had arranged they would stay, in a place she thought of as a refuge.

Ted opened the window of the automobile on his side to lean out, and Hilary said, "Ted, do be careful," and he drew back but kept his face close to the open window, so the wind blew his hair, exposing his high white forehead.

The narrow mountain road was empty and closed in on both sides by dark chestnut forest. Crested hoopoes flew from the forest on one side of the road into the forest on the other side, back and forth, higher and higher into the mountains.

The dirt road, level and smooth, curved along the edge of a valley, and round the curve were stone buildings that, from a distance, appeared to be a small village. Great white clouds were blown swiftly across the sky, causing shadows to flash over the village, which appeared to revolve slowly and separate into a big villa, a chapel, a walled-in garden, a long, stone, two-story house, stables, outhouses tangled in vines, and, beyond, chestnut forest. The passages among the buildings were paved in flat stones, weeds growing between them.

Hilary had insisted that Ted come to this place of refuge, where he would be attentive to where he was, and would come back to a world he seemed to have left, come back with her. She wanted him back.

They were among flowering broom, where she stopped to hold out a hand to the yellow bloom, perhaps to show them to Ted for his attention, and suddenly the bushes shook in a violent wind from nowhere, a squall, there where they were and nowhere else, as if the squall meant to isolate them in its buffeting. She put her hands to her mouth and nose and turned to Ted. He was holding his lowered head in his hands as if to steady himself against the violence of the wind. The squall, as suddenly as it rose, fell, and the bushes of broom became still. Hilary, smoothing her wind-blown hair, saw that Ted remained with his head lowered into his hands, and he continued, leaning forward in that position, Hilary staring at him. She could not call him; he might not have heard her. A strange sense came to her about him and that gesture, but she could not think of the sense as more than apprehensive, the gesture of a man for whom something was unbearable. When he did lower his hands, the sense stayed with her.

She asked, "Are you all right?" but he said nothing, and he walked on, and she followed.

In that strange sense of apprehension, she wanted him to follow her, and she hung back. If she called him, she thought, he might not answer, and would go on walking he himself did not know where. Her apprehension was about where he was going, not simply because they were in the mountains and there were cliffs and gorges, but because he didn't know where he was walking to, because her Ted was lost.

She called, "Ted," and he did turn round and walked slowly to her.

She led him to the garden she recalled from the past. On either side of the entrance stood listing obelisks. The old, shapeless rosebushes were entangled in bindweed. At the center of the garden was the stone basin of a fountain surrounded by a circular bench, and leaning over the basin, a plum tree. They stood side by side and she thought, Ted, Ted, because that was all she could think of about him, his name, Ted, Ted Beauchemin. Their standing together in the garden filled her with apprehension, and, as if he had a sense of it, he left her and the garden.

The path led to a man standing at the entrance of the stone villa, the double doors open. He showed them up a stairway with frescos of delicate flowers in delicate vases, through rooms with terra cotta–tiled floors freshly washed, the beams of the ceiling brushed, the walls plastered and whitewashed. The bedroom had only a large bed with an iron bedstead and pegs on the wall for clothes. The largest room had a stone sink into which spring water from a pipe over it flowed continuously, an old refectory table and rush-bottom chairs, and a rack on the wall with plates. There was a large demijohn of wine, a smaller of olive oil, and a screened-in food safe on the wall.

And the man excused himself, he must leave before the sun set, which in the mountains happened quickly.

And, yes, the sun set quickly. Two wide windows were open onto the night and flashing fireflies, some of which drifted into the room where they appeared and disappeared in the shadowed corners.

Because there was no light, Hilary was taken aback that Ted suggested to her that they go to bed, and in bed with him she felt that, because they were there because of him and she wasn't sure why, she should lie apart on the straw-filled mattress, the sheets rough, and she heard Ted breathe in his sleep.

She thought how strange that squall had been, how strange everything was. Since they had left London, since they had arrived in Italy, since they'd rented a car and they'd stopped in San Sepolcro to eat, ever since she had wanted to lean her head on the chest of the African. She had felt that something would happen, and it had, in that sudden burst of wind from nowhere.

She recalled Ted holding his head and she thought, Ted, Ted, her helpless Ted, who all his life had had to hold back from giving in, giving in, no, not to die—no, he did not want to die, but giving in to something greater than to want to die, but it was, yes, so much greater that there could only be a longing for it, a longing so helpless that Ted could only ever be at the edge of it overwhelming him, and though she could not help him with that, she loved him, yes, she loved Ted, for his tremendous longing.

She was woken by Ted getting up from the bed, and she heard him pee in a chamber pot, and he returned to the bed.

No, she thought, no, she had no idea what his tremendous longing was for, and she couldn't know because she was not Ted, and she did not believe in tremendous meanings, no, did not long for a tremendous meaning, but Ted did, and, yes, she loved him for that.

Unable to sleep, she slipped out of bed and put on a coat against the cold and went downstairs and lit an oil lamp.

Hilary thought she heard her name called from outside, from the sonorous midst of the crickets, and, apprehensive, she stood at one of the open windows to look out into darkness, where fireflies flashed everywhere. Her hands pressing the sill, she leaned further to look.

There were recollections that remained from as far back in her life as India and the hour of the cow dust in the evening. And here, now, was such a moment, here in this awareness of the night and the fireflies appearing and disappearing, forming constellations that soon fell apart but reformed into different constellations. She would find that recalling this moment would help her in her life.

When she did hear her name called, "Hilary," she quickly turned round back to the room, because the voice was Ted's calling her, but there was no one there. "Hilary," he called again, and she was bewildered, and on his calling her name once again, "Hilary," she turned back to the window and again leaned against the stone ledge to look out, and she saw him, there outside, where he was standing in the old walled garden, the walls fallen, the obelisks listing at each side of the entrance, the roses tangled in weeds, and fireflies forming constellations about him, and he was looking up to her, and he was smiling.

Fin

About the Author

David Plante grew up in Providence, Rhode Island, within a French-Canadian parish that was palisaded by its language, a French that dated from the time of the first French colonists in the early seventeenth century to what was then most of North America, la Nouvelle France. His background was very similar to that of Jack Kerouac, who was brought up in a French-speaking parish in Lowell, Massachusetts. Plante has been inspired to write novels rooted in La Nouvelle France, most notably in *The Family*, a contender for the National Book Award. His renowned book, *Difficult Women*, a non-fiction work that profiled Jean Rhys, Sonia Orwell, and Germaine Greer, was reissued by *The New York Review of Books Press* in 2017. He has dual nationality, American and British, but lives in Lucca, Italy.